★ "With timely, important anecdotes that ring painfully true, Firestone cuts to the heart of the damage that dress coding can inflict . . . [A] deeply satisfying, variously inclusive journey with a wonderfully flawed main character."
—*PUBLISHERS WEEKLY*, starred review

"With a perfect mix of friendship, humor, and girl power, *Dress Coded* is a book readers need."
—STACY MCANULTY, bestselling author of *The Miscalculations of Lightning Girl*

"An electrifying ode to the power of standing up and standing together."
—ANNE URSU, author of *The Real Boy* and *The Lost Girl*

"The story reflects the ups and downs of middle school, and the validation that comes when one successfully stands up for what one believes."
—*SCHOOL LIBRARY CONNECTION*

ALSO BY CARRIE FIRESTONE

The First Rule of Climate Club

CARRIE FIRESTONE

putnam

G. P. PUTNAM'S SONS

G. P. PUTNAM'S SONS

An imprint of Penguin Random House LLC, New York

First published in the United States of America by G. P. Putnam's Sons,
an imprint of Penguin Random House LLC, 2020
First paperback edition published 2022

G. P. Putnam's Sons is a registered trademark of Penguin Random House LLC.
Penguin Books & colophon are registered trademarks of Penguin Books Limited.

Visit us online at penguinrandomhouse.com

THE LIBRARY OF CONGRESS HAS CATALOGED THE HARDCOVER EDITION AS FOLLOWS:
Names: Firestone, Carrie, author.
Title: Dress coded / Carrie Firestone.
Description: New York: G. P. Putnam's Sons, [2020]
Summary: "An eighth grader starts a podcast to protest the unfair dress code
enforcement at her middle school and sparks a rebellion"—Provided by publisher.
Identifiers: LCCN 2019033840 | ISBN 9781984816436 (hardcover) | ISBN 9781984816443
Subjects: CYAC: Dress codes—Fiction. | Protest movements—Fiction. | Middle schools—Fiction.
Schools—Fiction. | Podcasts—Fiction.
Classification: LCC PZ7.1.F55 Dr 2020 | DDC [Fic]—dc23
LC record available at https://lccn.loc.gov/2019033840

Printed in the United States of America

ISBN 9781984816450

1st Printing

LSCH

Design by Suki Boynton
Text set in Adobe Garamond Pro

For the unlikely rule breakers
The ones who keep going
The ones who change minds

DRESS CODED: A PODCAST

EPISODE ONE

This is my first podcast and I have no idea what I'm doing. I've only listened to two podcasts in my life; one was about famous guitarists, and the other was about Southern cooking. Neither prepared me for what I'm about to say. But I feel like this is the best way to tell the real story about what happened to make the entire Fisher Middle School eighth grade hate Olivia Bonaventura.

It's time for the truth.

ME: My name is Molly Frost, and this is episode one of *Dress Coded: A Podcast*, the real story behind the dress-code disaster at Fisher Middle School. The whole incident happened in the Fisher flower garden, right next to the mountain of kindness rocks, Mrs. Tucker's pet project. I was there. I saw the whole thing. And now I'm sitting here with Olivia. Hi, Olivia, do you want to give the background?

OLIVIA: You can give the background, Molly.

ME: Are you sure? It's your story.

OLIVIA: You were a witness.

ME: Okay, well, it all began last Wednesday. I woke up late in a panic because I was already missing first period and my mom was at an appointment, so I had to cut through the woods to the back path of our school. When I got

1

to the garden, which, for you non-Fisher listeners, was planted to honor the six Fisher graduates who died in wars, I stopped to tie my shoe. I looked up, and that's when I saw you standing in front of Mr. Dern and Dr. Couchman. I still remember Dr. Couchman's face was bright red and Mr. Dern was pointing his finger at you, and you were crying.

Silence.

OLIVIA: Molly, can you pause it for a minute?

I'm already beginning to think *Dress Coded: A Podcast* was a mistake. Olivia seems very uncomfortable.

"Are you okay?" I say, checking to make sure the recorder is off.

She nods. "Maybe we should just forget about this. Pearl says the story will die by high school graduation."

"Olivia, I can't let everyone hate you for something that wasn't your fault. It's just not right. People need to know what happened."

I don't say this to Olivia, for obvious reasons, but when Mr. Dern and Dr. Couchman were yelling at her because of a royal-blue tank top with spaghetti straps, I witnessed a piece of her soul leave her body. Until that day, I had thought souls left bodies at the time of death, all at once. But when I saw Olivia's face, her arms crossed in front of her, the tears streaming down her cheeks, and the rose-colored hives blooming upward and outward across her chest, I knew everything I had ever believed about souls leaving bodies was wrong. Souls leave bodies in tiny gasps, like when you hold the lip of a balloon tightly and let out the air a little bit at a time.

That's why I texted her two days later. I had planned to talk to her at school, but she refused to go.

LETTER TO FOURTH GRADERS

If I could write a letter to my fourth-grade class, I would keep it short, because we didn't have long attention spans in fourth grade. I would say this:

Dear Fourth Graders,

I know you all think boob *is a funny word, and it is. But it won't be for long. Okay, maybe it will still be funny for the boys in eighth grade. But for eighth-grade girls, there's nothing funny about boobs. They hurt sometimes when they're growing, and they don't always grow in evenly, and sometimes they grow in all at once. It is possible to go visit your grandma in Florida for spring break and come back with big lumps of flesh poking through your shirt, and before you know it, you're standing in a garden while two grown men yell at you and make you cry because your shirt no longer fits. And if that's not your story, you may wake up every single day, peek down your shirt, close your eyes tight, open them, and then look to see if anything has popped up overnight. And when it hasn't, you will put on the bra you don't need and wear a baggy shirt, because you don't want people to notice you still look like a fourth grader (no offense). And then you and your friend with the big lumps of flesh will walk around in your ill-fitting shirts with your shoulders rounded because you have grown to hate the word you once thought was so funny.* Boob. *The biggest four-letter word of middle school.*

I used to be better friends with Olivia and Pearl.

Olivia was in my fifth-grade class, and Pearl was in my sixth-grade class. They were both lunch-table friends, as opposed to sleepover friends or the even closer double-sleepover friends. We talked about homework and sat together at assemblies and picked each other first (or at least second or third) for teams at recess. I knew Olivia had a secret crush on Rahul, and Pearl and I fake-dated a few of the same boys. Fake-dating in fifth and sixth grade means telling everyone you're dating, then making sure you don't make eye contact with your fake boyfriend until you break up a week later.

I'll never forget the time Nick was about to pull the chair out from under me just as I was sitting down and Olivia punched him and saved me from falling. She got sent to the office for that and I felt really bad, but she assured me it was worth it.

I lost touch with Olivia in seventh grade because I hadn't seen much of her in sixth grade and because Olivia got into seventh-grade honors. I lost touch with Pearl because Pearl isn't allowed to have Snapchat, which kind of makes her a social outcast (I wish it didn't have to be that way), and because Pearl also got into honors.

I didn't get into honors because I'm a pretty average person in every way. I wouldn't say I try my best at school, lacrosse, clarinet, or life in general. But compared to my brother, Danny, I'm a rock star.

Pearl and Olivia are pretty good friends. If I had to guess (because I haven't really talked much to Pearl *or* Olivia this year), they're sit-on-the-bus-together-on-field-trips friends and *maybe* sleepover friends, but probably not double-sleepover friends.

I hung out with my lacrosse team for a while in seventh grade, because it was easy to make plans after practice and half of us still weren't allowed to use our phones unless it was for an emergency, so making plans in person was our only option.

I can assure you our forbidden phones were ringing off the hook when Fisher Middle School went into active-shooter lockdown last spring. Mrs. Pullman thought she heard Chris Reynolds say he was hiding a bomb. We're still not sure if he actually said that, but we went on lockdown and Chris Reynolds got suspended. My mom has said "I love you, Molly" at drop-off every morning since that day, even when she's in a miserable mood because of Danny. At least twice a month, she'll remind me: "If there's a shooter, *don't* necessarily do what the teachers tell you to do. Listen to your gut. Run if your gut tells you to run. Hide if your gut tells you to hide." I don't really trust my gut, but I don't tell her that.

Since eighth grade started, Navya, Ashley, and Bea have been my closest friends. They're not in honors either, but Navya is the best lacrosse player on the team, Bea is so talented at art she gets fifty dollars a day face-painting at birthday parties, and Ashley has a pool and a hot tub. They like hanging out with me because I'm funny.

That's pretty much all anyone needs to know about what my life was like before I saw Olivia getting dress coded in the Kindness Garden while Pearl stood there holding a pair of Pink sweatpants.

Oh, I did want to mention my brother, Danny, has been sucking up all my parents' energy, because he's addicted to vaping. In their free time, my parents enjoy searching Danny's room and backpack, hiding their cash so Danny can't take it to buy pods, and calling doctors to ask how long it will be before Danny gets popcorn lung and dies.

I know at least twenty kids in the eighth grade who have gotten vaping pods from Danny.

That's how he gets his cash.

He doesn't need Mom and Dad's money.

LETTER TO PARENTS

Dear FMS Parents:

It is with deep regret that I write to inform you our camping trip to Strawberry Hill State Park has been canceled. As you will recall, I sent out a letter on February 25 promising a wonderful trip if our eighth graders simply followed the dress code outlined in the student handbook. For the better part of the semester, your children have done a fantastic job. Recently, however, a student violated the dress code and after we gave her ample opportunity to comply, she refused. Unfortunately, rules are rules.

In an effort to provide a safe, distraction-free learning environment, we encourage your children to continue following the policy stated in our FMS hand-book. Thank you for your attention to this matter. We apologize for any inconvenience this may have caused your family.

Sincerely,
Jim Couchman, EdD

WILL'S TEXTS

My best friend Will texts me: **I hate camping, but that was messed up. I thought Olivia was normal.**

Will is my neighbor. Our backyards touch, and our dads built the tree house when we were eight and inseparable. I barely see him anymore because he's addicted to some video game I've never heard of and because our parents don't hang out as much since my mom is stressed-out about Danny.

Our moms always say, "If you two don't manage to get prom dates, you can always go together." They've been saying this since back when Will and I routinely wrestled each other to the ground over a sippy cup full of Goldfish.

"It's not like when you went to the prom," I tell my mom. "Nobody cares. I may go with a boy, or a girl, or a group."

That's when she tilts her head a little and rests her hand on my leg and says, "Are you bisexual, Molly? Because that's totally and completely fine."

"Where did you get 'Are you bisexual?' from 'I may or may not have a date to the prom'?" I ask.

We've had this conversation at least five times.

I text Will back. **What is that supposed to mean? How is Olivia not normal?**

Will replies, If she were normal she wouldn't be trying to get attention.

I'm too angry to reply.

"Why don't we try a different approach this time? I'll give a little background, and then I'll ask you questions and you can just answer them."

"That works," Olivia says, leaning back against the exposed tree trunk.

ME: Hello, Fisher Middle School and beyond. My name is Molly Frost, and this is *Dress Coded: A Podcast*. I'm here with Olivia. She was recently yelled at for wearing a tank top at school. As many of you know, back in February, Fisher Middle School administrators made an agreement with the eighth grade. If we could go the rest of the school year without anyone getting dress coded, Dr. Couchman would take us on a camping trip to Strawberry Hill State Park. So after he humiliated Olivia, Dr. Couchman announced that the camping trip was canceled because a young lady had decided to selfishly violate the dress code. One of our classmates (you know who you are, Jack Reese) overheard Dr. Couchman talking to Mrs. Peabody about it and told the whole school Olivia was the one who ruined our camping trip.

I pause the recorder and look at Olivia. She gives me a thumbs-up.

ME: I am here to tell you there are two sides to every story, and I, as a witness to the event, believe Olivia should be able to tell hers. So I have invited her to join me here today.

We hear a creaking noise, and I pause the recorder again. It's Pearl pushing on the hatch door of the tree house. "Where were you?" I ask.

"Tennis," she says. She takes a seat next to Olivia and picks up a ginger cookie. I wanted to make Olivia comfortable for the second take, so I cleaned the tree house, put a few more pillows around to warm it up, and brought up some cookies and glasses of lemonade with our new stainless-steel straws.

I press my finger to my lips, because I can tell Pearl is about to start talking.

ME: Olivia, welcome and thank you for agreeing to take part in *Dress Coded: A Podcast*. Before you tell us what happened, maybe you could give us a little background. Have you ever been dress coded before?

OLIVIA: Yes. Fingertip has given me a bunch of warnings, and Miss Wells dress coded me last year because my gym shorts were too short.

ME: Not surprising. And what happened?

OLIVIA: She pulled me over and told me to go to the office,

13

and I asked if I could just go change into my regular shorts, and she said fine but told me not to wear those gym shorts again.

ME: And how did that make you feel?

OLIVIA: Annoyed, because it started pouring when we were running on the track and I had to walk around the rest of the day in soggy shorts.

ME: That's the worst. I'm sorry you had to deal with that. So other than dealing with dress coding, how do you feel about school?

OLIVIA: Pretty neutral. I'm trying to focus on science, because I'm going to a STEM camp this summer.

ME: Oh, that's cool. Okay, let's get right to it. I've invited another witness to join us. Say hi, Pearl.

PEARL: Hi.

ME: Pearl will comment later in the podcast. But first, would you like to tell us what happened, Olivia?

Olivia takes a deep breath and pulls a cookie apart, dropping crumbs all over the pink plastic table my cousin Shannon gave us after Dad built the tree house.

OLIVIA: I was walking to my locker from math with a hall pass. I wasn't even thinking about the fact that I was wearing a tank top. I needed to get my phone to call my sister and see if she could bring me something.

ME: Do you want to tell us what you needed her to bring you?

She shakes her head and mouths, *No*.

OLIVIA: No, that's fine. So I was walking to the south hallway, and I saw Dr. Couchman out of the corner of my eye. He kept calling "Hey," but I didn't slow down. We all know Dr. Couchman only knows the names of the baseball players. He finally ran up behind me and tapped me on the shoulder and asked me to step outside. I got really nervous. Mr. Dern was sitting in his classroom, and Couchman knocked on his window and waved him outside. That's when they both started telling me I was in violation of the dress code, and asking why would I be so selfish, and did I realize everyone else had gone over eight weeks without violating the dress code and I'd ruined the chance for our grade to go on the camping trip.

ME: How did you react?

OLIVIA: I freaked out. I begged them to give me another chance. Couchman said he'd consider it if I put my sweatshirt on and promised to never do it again.

ME: So did you?

She looks down at her lap and folds her hands.

OLIVIA: No. I told them I couldn't, that I needed to keep my sweatshirt tied around my waist. They told me I was disobeying the rules and being disrespectful, and they made me go to the office and call my parents.

ME: What did your parents say?

OLIVIA: They both work, and they couldn't come all the way here to pick me up. So I called my sister. She left high school, picked me up, took me home, and went back out to get me Starbucks iced tea and a giant chocolate chip cookie, which was nice of her. Then she got in big trouble for leaving school.

I'm stuck on feeling jealous that Olivia's sister was nice enough to pick her up, buy her Starbucks, and get in trouble for her. Danny would never do that for me.

ME: Olivia, now I need to ask you a question, and it's going to be really embarrassing.

She stares at me. I wish I could say I know how she feels, but I can't. I can only imagine how she feels because, as my mom says, I'm a late bloomer. I have the body of a nine-year-old.

Pearl stands next to Olivia and puts her hand on Olivia's shoulder.

OLIVIA: Can we just stop now? I'd rather be hated by the whole grade than talk about this.

I don't blame her.

ME: Yeah. We can stop.

DEFINITIONS

PULLOVER *(noun)*

a garment, especially a sweater or jacket, put on over the head and covering the top half of the body

PULL OVER *(verb phrase)*

1. to move a vehicle or its driver to the side of or off the road
2. to target a Fisher Middle School student for the purpose of calling out her manner of dress when said student is violating one or more rules on the dress-code page of the Fisher Middle School handbook

Examples:

I tied my pullover around my waist.

Fingertip pulled me over because my bra strap was showing.

My teacher pulled me over because my knee was distracting him.

A BRIEF HISTORY OF FISHER MIDDLE SCHOOL'S DRESS CODE

"I really appreciate you trying to help me, but let's just forget it," Olivia says. "I'm honestly thinking about begging my parents to let me be homeschooled."

Pearl and I look at each other.

Then Pearl says, "I accidentally left the rubber bands from my braces on a paper towel in art class last year, and Nick told everyone I was nasty, and I begged my parents to homeschool me."

"Nick is nasty," I say.

We eat cookies and stare out the window. This is the first time I've used the tree house in a while.

"I have one more thought," I say.

"Why are you trying so hard, Molly?" Olivia looks at me with dead-serious eyes. "Like, we're barely friends anymore."

"Because what they did to you isn't right. And their little plot to get us to do what they want by offering a camping trip is not right either."

We hadn't had dress codes in elementary school, so when we got to Fisher Middle School, they gave us a student handbook outlining all the things we couldn't wear.

The summer before seventh grade, my friend Liza and I went shopping at Forever 21, which was a big deal, because until then my mom was all about Target and Old Navy. I picked out really cute shorts and a purple tank top, and Liza got the same shorts with a green tank top, to complement her eyes (we didn't want to be too matchy). Our moms let us buy expensive white high-tops and Lokai bracelets, and after all that practicing, we finally got to wear a little makeup in public.

We felt beautiful.

Liza got dress coded the very first day of seventh grade, before they even gave us the handbooks, before we even knew how to get to our classrooms. I wasn't there to see it, but I heard Fingertip chased Liza down the hall and made her extend her arms, and pointed out that her shorts were shorter than where her fingertips landed and said that was not allowed at this school. I heard Liza bit her lip so hard it bled. She was trying not to cry.

I spent my first day of middle school hiding from teachers because I was wearing the exact same shorts as Liza. My friends didn't think I would have as much of a problem, because my behind was much smaller than Liza's. That didn't seem fair.

Liza and I didn't tell our moms about the dress code. We didn't want them to be furious that they had spent all that money on shorts and tank tops that we weren't even going to wear to school. Liza had to wear her sixth-grade clothes, which were way too small, and she got detention three times that year because of tight clothing.

"So what do you think we should do?" Olivia says.

"Let's scrap the podcast and invite Bea, Ashley, and

Navya over to the tree house and tell them the story privately," I say. "They're reasonable people, and I think they can help."

"Ugh," Olivia says. "Fine. Why not? I'm going to be homeschooled next year anyway."

FINGERTIP

We don't know her real name.

She calls herself the dean of students, but nobody has ever seen her do anything but stare at girls, search for a rogue bra strap or a bare shoulder, and bark out warnings. Some girls get six or seven warnings a day—this is because Fingertip doesn't remember if she's already given someone a warning.

It has become a rite of passage on the first day of school. Eighth-grade girls warn seventh-grade girls to stay away, run away, sneak away from Fingertip, dean of dress coding.

Fingertip is most famous for the act of making girls stand still and extend their arms straight so she can decide if their fingertips fall below their shorts (which almost always happens, because no stores sell shorts that long).

So life at Fisher Middle is a pulling game. When you see Fingertip, pull down your shorts. But don't pull them down too low, or your stomach will show. It's better if you learn her pattern so you can avoid her altogether. But if she does get you, *don't talk back*.

She has her favorite targets—the bigger girls, the girls with boobs and butts, the prettiest girls, and the girls with long legs.

Nobody has ever seen her stop a boy.

Some people believe Fingertip is a robot with a bob haircut, orthopedic shoes, and a grubby old burgundy sweater she sometimes makes people wear if they can't change their clothes in a timely manner, and that Dr. Couchman programmed her to say seven things:

1. Extend your arms.
2. Bra strap.
3. This is a warning.
4. Pull it up.
5. Pull it down.
6. What's it going to take to get you girls to listen?
7. Down to the office. Now.

Robot or human, Fingertip and her sweater are as popular at Fisher Middle School as Mondays, math tests, and mold on the hamburger buns.

IT'S OKAY TO TRICK YOUR FRIENDS
IF IT'S FOR A GOOD CAUSE

I bribe my friends with pizza. I don't tell them why I need them to drop everything and get over to my house.

I don't have money and my parents are at Dad's work dinner, so I make Danny order with the selling-vaping-supplies-to-middle-schoolers money. It feels gross, because I'm about to feed my friends crime-money pizza, but it's for the greater good.

"I need to go. I have a lot of homework," Pearl says.

I know Pearl feels guilty. If she had offered her sweatpants right away, instead of hesitating, going to her locker, and *then* running around the school looking for Olivia, none of this would have happened.

"Just do the homework here," I say. "We won't bother you."

Olivia and I lie on the floor, watching a pack of nervous birds going back and forth between our tree and another tree. Pearl is sticking her tongue out, trying to concentrate on math.

"Do you resent your boobs?" I say, pointing at Olivia's chest.

"Yes. Do you resent not having boobs?" she says.

"Yes."

She laughs. "Remember when nobody had boobs and we could just focus on fake-dating boys at recess?"

"Those were the days."

A loud thump makes us jump. Somebody is banging on the tree-house floor.

I pull the rope, and the door squeaks open. Ashley pokes her head through and climbs in. Her face drops. She looks confused, like our dog, Thibodeaux, when my cousin's parrot barks back at him.

"Wait, what?" Ashley says, looking down at Navya and Bea, who are coming up behind her.

"Calm down and just get in here," I say.

They ball up their fists and stand in the corner—well, half stand, because the ceilings are a little too low for us now.

"Sit," I order. I'm not sure where I'm getting this new bossy attitude. I think those two minutes in the garden, witnessing Couchman and Dern humiliate my old friend, permanently altered my DNA.

"Hey, guys," Pearl says, closing her math book and stuffing it in her backpack.

My friends' first thought is most likely: *Why is Pearl here in Molly's tree house with the girl who ruined eighth grade?*

"Women, I brought you here to clear things up. I know stuff. Pearl knows stuff. Olivia is innocent. And the real villains here are Couchman and his little henchman, Dern."

I should write fairy tales.

"Okaaaaay," Navya says. She can be difficult when she's mad and in a confined space.

"Sit down," I say.

And they do.

THE LIST OF THINGS WE HAD PLANNED TO DO ON THE EIGHTH-GRADE CAMPING TRIP TO STRAWBERRY HILL STATE PARK

1. Sneak out of our tent and meet in the woods to play truth or dare with the baseball boys (specific to Ashley, because the rest of us don't like the baseball boys).
2. Wear whatever we want, because the dress-code agreement will be over.
3. Eat as many bags of gummy candy as possible (specific to Bea, who will get her braces off a few days before the camping trip).
4. Swim in the lake at midnight.
5. Try to stay up until morning.

THE FIRST THING WE HAD PLANNED
TO DO ON THE BIG PACKAGE WAS THE
TRIP TO STRAWBERRY HILL.

MY PLAN WORKS

It doesn't take much convincing after I tell Ashley, Navya, and Bea what I saw and then Pearl tells how she had tapped Olivia on the shoulder as she was getting up from science and whispered in her ear something no girl ever wants to hear. Olivia tells how embarrassed she was and how she was going to go to the nurse, but she was afraid a boy might be there getting an ear check or a Band-Aid, so she rushed to her locker to get her phone and call her sister to bring her new pants. Then Pearl tells how she remembered she had new Pink sweatpants in her locker, so she grabbed them and went running around the school looking for Olivia. That's when she saw Couchman pull Olivia out to the garden.

By the end of my explanation, Navya, Ashley, and Bea are hugging Olivia, the real kind of hugging that squeezes your breath out of you for a few seconds.

"We can do our own camping trip," Bea says. "It's not like he was taking us to Europe."

"You know why he did this, right?" I say. "He bribed us so we would do what he wants like good little children. And it worked. We fell for it."

"I guarantee he had Fingertip roaming the halls even

more, looking for somebody to dress code so he didn't have to take us on the trip," Navya says.

"Olivia, you were a sacrificial lamb," Pearl says.

"What's that?" Ashley says.

Pearl looks confused. "I'm not a hundred percent sure."

DANNY BRINGS THE PIZZA

We go on venting about Couchman and Dern and the other teachers who have made our lives miserable since seventh grade. Danny texts that he's been calling up to us and can we please get the Danny's-favorite-curse-word-that-I-won't-repeat pizza?

Watch your tone, I text back. **I know stuff.**

Holding incriminating information over Danny has given me a lot of power.

Bea and Navya climb halfway down the ladder and grab the pizza and a two-liter of Sprite from my brother, who shoves it at them and storms away. I don't know if Olivia or Pearl are aware of his "dealings," so I keep my mouth shut about it.

Some of the girls on our lacrosse team vape. I want to take them home and hide them in my mom's closet and make them watch her cry herself to sleep, worrying about my brother. Then maybe they'd stop. But who knows? Kids don't always care about their parents' feelings.

"What grade is Danny in now?" Pearl asks.

"Eleventh."

"Does he still hate you?"

"I don't know," I say before changing the subject.

We inhale the pizza and take turns trying not to backwash into the Sprite bottle, because Danny wasn't considerate enough to bring cups.

"So can we get everyone to stop hating Olivia?" I ask.

They all say yes.

"It's a biological function," Navya says. "It happens to everyone."

"Not everyone," Olivia says.

"Okay, half of everyone."

"What if instead of a podcast—which is seriously embarrassing, Molly—we just start a whisper campaign?" Bea asks.

"What's that?" I say.

"We just quietly start telling girls we know, until it eventually gets out. And, yes, Olivia, it's still embarrassing, but even the boys will understand the position you were in."

"They have moms," Pearl says.

I think we may have worn Olivia down. I'm pretty sure she wants to get back to science and her normal life. "And the good thing is, summer is coming and nobody will know about this at your STEM camp," I say.

Olivia's face seems to relax a little with that comment. "Go ahead. Do the whisper campaign."

We've just gotten permission to gossip, which is a very liberating feeling.

Navya eats all the cheese off Bea's pizza, and Bea eats Navya's crusts. That's some serious friendship.

Olivia gets another big group hug before everyone goes home to wash dirty lacrosse clothes or eat ice cream or study for math or fume about the dress code. I'm fuming at myself for letting a camping trip cloud my judgment.

LUNCH BUNCH

Pearl isn't the only one who asks if Danny still hates me. Things got bad when Danny started middle school. Things were always a little bad—he was never nice to me or my parents or Tibby or anyone, really. But he had his good days and bad days. Middle school for Danny was all bad days.

Mom got calls to pick him up for fighting, for mouthing off to teachers, for cursing. I can't remember all of it. That's when I started hiding in my room.

In fifth grade, Ms. Mary, the school counselor, invited me to the mysterious Lunch Bunch. She said it was a special invitation and we would get pizza delivered and two ice cream cups each. We played board games and listened to any song we wanted and hung out with other specially chosen kids. It was the best part of every Friday.

At first, we talked about family vacations and shows we liked to watch. Then Ms. Mary told us about how her friend was dealing with cancer, and Jack Reese started talking about his dad's cancer. Then Ms. Mary told us about two famous people getting divorced, and this kid Alex talked about his parents' divorce, and then Ms. Mary talked about how annoying her big brother was, and I blurted out all the things Danny was doing to make our house noisy and stressful and sad.

Olivia was at Lunch Bunch sometimes. Her parents were getting divorced too. Her mom and Alex's mom had the same lawyer. Olivia beat me at Connect 4 literally every time.

One Friday morning before school, Mom asked me if I had made my lunch yet.

"I don't need to make it. I have Lunch Bunch," I said.

Danny stopped chewing his bagel and said with his mouth full, "You're in Lunch Bunch? That's for mental cases." He turned to Mom. "Why is she in Lunch Bunch?"

Mom grabbed his arm and squeezed. "You will not talk like that." Spit came out of her mouth she was so furious.

"Talk like what? Lunch Bunch is for crazy people."

It all hit me. Lunch Bunch wasn't for special kids. It was for troubled kids.

The kid whose dad has cancer. The kids whose parents are getting divorced. The kid whose brother is destroying her family.

I never went to Lunch Bunch again.

BY NINE O'CLOCK IN THE MORNING

It's nine o'clock in the morning, and the whispers from the whisper campaign are louder than our marching band's Memorial Day parade rehearsal.

And now the entire school knows: Olivia needed to tie her sweatshirt around her waist to hide the giant period bloodstain on her new white jeans. When Couchman saw her, she was going to call her sister to ask her to bring new pants. When Couchman told her to put her sweatshirt on, because he couldn't handle seeing her shoulders, she told him *no*.

Everyone understood why.

Olivia got hugs and knowing glances and sympathetic smiles all day from the girls. She got silence from the boys. Dead silence.

But in middle school, when you're dealing with something as horrifying as period on pants, silence from boys is a dream come true.

TALKING TO A SEVENTH GRADER
ABOUT A DIFFICULT TOPIC

The high school and the middle school share a bus. I've already explained one of the obvious reasons that it is not a good idea (Danny selling pods to twelve-year-olds).

On the first day of school this year, I saw my neighbor down the street standing in the bus line, looking like she was going to throw up.

"Are you sick, Mary Kate?" I asked her.

"I think so," she said.

Mary Kate is a year younger than me and we are good neighborhood friends, but she's sheltered. Her parents don't let her watch TV, much less own a phone. I understand there are a lot of scary things out there, but sheltering a kid that much is going to end up backfiring. For example, she'll be so terrified to ride on a bus full of older kids, she might just puke.

Mary Kate has been sitting next to me on the bus ride home ever since that day.

"Toad, do you have any food?" Danny says to Mary Kate. He calls her Toad, and me Frog. We have no idea why.

"No," she says. When he's not looking, she slides her hand into the front pocket of her backpack and hands me a slightly melted Reese's Peanut Butter Cup.

"Is it true about that girl Olivia getting her thingy and,

like, having an accident and getting dress coded in the middle of it?" Mary Kate asks me.

"Yeah. It's all true. Pretty awful, huh?"

"Does that happen a lot?"

"Dress coding? It did every minute of every day until they came up with that stupid camping-trip bribe."

"No. I mean accidents." Mary Kate looks terrified again. I'm pretty confident she would rather suffocate slowly in a vat of peanut butter than stain her pants in school.

I don't have the heart to tell her I'm no expert. "No. Not at all. But keep a spare pair of sweatpants in your locker at all times, just to be safe."

"I will."

Danny reaches across the aisle and waves a twenty-dollar bill in Mary Kate's face. "I see you eating, Toad. Twenty bucks for one peanut butter cup."

"I'm all out." Mary Kate is also terrified of people who vape.

Danny pulls a flash-drive-shaped device out of his pocket and sucks in the vapor. It disgusts me.

The seventh grader next to him, a kid named Ted, elbows Danny to share. Danny holds it up to Ted's mouth, and Ted sucks in.

Frog and Toad are so disgusted we can't even finish our peanut butter cups.

IF YOU'RE NOT A BIG FISH, YOUR MOM WON'T FEEL LIKE FRYING YOU

My mom treats Danny like he's a toddler, which is why she felt the need to quit her job at the food bank last year to go back to being a full-time parent.

She loved that job.

"Hi, honey. How was your day?" she says, trying to get close enough to sniff Danny's clothes for traces of mango or mint, the most popular vaping flavors.

"Good," Danny says, wiggling away from her as he flings open the pantry. Danny is beginning to learn that if he just says "Good" and doesn't give her attitude, she'll leave him alone.

"How about you, Molly Mae?" Luckily, she doesn't feel the need to sniff me. "How was your math test?"

"Fine." I search the fridge for milk to wash down my peanut butter cup. Thibodeaux flings himself at me, and I toss him a biscuit from the Tibby treat jar.

"Has everyone recovered from the camping-trip news? Daddy was bummed it was canceled. He just ordered you a really cool LED flashlight." She watches Danny walk up the stairs.

"Don't you think it's a little ridiculous that they canceled the trip after one dress-code incident?" I say.

"Well, it was kind of an incentive thing. I see what they were trying to do, and as the principal said, rules are rules."

She moves in and stands close. "Did he vape on the way home?" she whispers, her hot breath tickling my ear.

"Not that I saw," I lie. I wish she would focus on my life for once. "I don't even care about the camping trip."

"Really? But you've been looking forward to it all spring."

"I think the dress coding at our school is out of control. Can you go in and talk to the principal about how wrong it is to walk around school policing what people wear? Specifically, policing what girls wear?"

She looks at me in a that-is-not-a-normal-Molly-thing-to-say way. "I think we've got bigger fish to fry, hon. And besides, in a few weeks you'll be on your way to high school. I've heard they're much more lenient about dress coding there. Maybe too lenient."

"Now that the camping trip is canceled, can I just wear whatever I want?"

"Why would you ask for trouble?"

"Because I want to take a stand on something for once in my life."

She tilts her head and is probably thinking, *Who are you, and what have you done to my child? She's not upset about the camping trip,* and *she wants to take a stand on something?*

"You know what, Molly? I would be okay with that. As long as you're covering your tush, of course."

"So if you get a call to bring me clothes, you won't be mad?"

"No. I won't be mad. I'll tell them my daughter is dressed just fine. How about that?"

"Thanks, Mom."

"I'm proud of you, hon."

Sometimes you need to fry the little fish too.

GILBERT PETTIBONES WAFFLE THE THIRD

Bea and I were forced to be friends on a rainy October morning in first grade, when all the classes lined up for the field-trip bus and we had the bad luck of being the only two girls in our bus group. We panicked, stared at each other, and, without saying a word, sat together. At first, we stared straight ahead because I didn't know her name and she didn't know mine. But then she offered me a sugar cookie from her brown-bag lunch, and I offered her chips from my brown-bag lunch.

"Be-uh?" I said, looking at the name written on her brown bag.

"Bee," she said. "Like *buzzzzzzzzz*."

We giggled, because that's what first graders do.

We held hands and followed the teacher around the village, watching people dressed up like colonists weave on looms and knead dough and teach us about herbs in the medicine garden.

"Look, a tiny mouse," Bea said. And she scooped up the mouse, a baby for sure, because it was the size of a first grader's thumb, and held it quivering in her hand. We put it in my brown bag (after I took out the sandwich and the rest of the chips), and we made it a bed of grass and leaves.

Our teacher wouldn't let us keep the mouse, even though we had big plans of sharing it forever. "I'll take him one week; you take him the next week," Bea had said.

We released the tiny mouse back into the medicine garden, right under the sage plant where we'd found him. "He probably has a mom who would miss him, anyway," I said. Bea was busy drawing on her brown bag.

"There," she said when she was done. "Now we'll remember him."

The picture looked just like the mouse. I was impressed.

"Let's give him a name," I said.

We named him Gilbert Pettibones Waffle the Third. I don't remember where we got that name. But I do remember thinking Bea would be a good person to have around.

I was right.

DRESS CODED: A PODCAST

EPISODE ONE (TAKE THREE)

ME: My name is Molly Frost, and this is *Dress Coded: A Podcast.* I've decided to speak out on the issue of school dress coding after my friend was humiliated by the principal of our middle school for wearing a tank top that exposed her shoulders. In my opinion, it is wrong to do this to a thirteen-year-old girl. I have invited guests to talk about the issue of dress coding in middle school. Today, I welcome Bea M., renowned local artist, to tell us what happened to her last year in seventh grade. Bea, first tell us a little about yourself.

BEA: Well, I'm really into art, especially painting, although I'm starting to like sculpture. This summer, I'm going to Italy with my dad, and I'm really excited about that. I've never been out of the country. And, I don't know, that's about it. Oh, also I'm the only person in my friend group obsessed with K-pop.

ME: I don't mind K-pop.

BEA: You *don't mind* K-pop. I'm *obsessed* with K-pop.

ME: That's true. Okay, let's get to the topic of dress coding in middle school. Have you ever been dress coded, and if so, what was your experience?

BEA: I was thinking about this on the way over here, and honestly, I've been harassed in the hallways and in

39

class, like, dozens of times, but I've only had to go to the office once.

ME: When you say harassed dozens of times, can you explain what that means?

BEA: Oh my gosh, it's so annoying. Last year, at the beginning of seventh grade, it was impossible to find shorts longer than my fingertips. My arms are freakishly long, and the stores only sell shorter shorts. My mom was getting so irritated. She had bought me a few pairs of shorts for the beginning of the year because the school district is too cheap to get air-conditioning. And literally every day as I was walking to class, Fingertip would call out, "Hey, you gotta pull down those shorts or don't wear them again." And I would try to yank on the shorts while I was carrying all my stuff and trying to figure out how to get to class, because everything was so confusing. And then sometimes Couchman would stop me and flash the handbook in my face and give me a "warning" and make me late for class. This happened so many times I can't count.

ME: So what were you wearing to get called down to the office?

BEA: The same exact shorts as everyone else. The only difference was that these had rips in the front. I was in tech ed, and Mr. Schwab was looking at me like I was a dead bug squished on someone's shoe. He called me to the front of the room and asked the class if I was going to church, because I looked so "holey." Then he called the office and told them he was sending me down for a dress-code violation. They called my mom, and she was so furious because she was sick of trying to find long enough shorts. So she brought in *her* shorts, and I had to walk around wearing beige mom shorts all day. After that, I just boiled to death in pants until the weather got cooler.

ME: Bea, I'm really sorry I made fun of you that day you were wearing your mom's shorts.

BEA: Molly, you're only human.

TREEHOUSE SLIME FACTORY

If you asked me to tell you about fifth grade, I probably wouldn't remember much. That's because that entire year was dominated by slime. Will found out about it from his cousin in Baltimore and made his mom buy all the ingredients—borax, glue, shaving cream, contact lens solution, and containers—and dump them off in our tree house.

I was skeptical.

"You're just going to mess up the tree house and leave all this stuff here for me to clean up," I said to Will. But he was already on the floor watching a YouTube video on slime, with a big plastic bowl and the strange combination of ingredients surrounding him.

The first batch was a bit off. The second batch was better. The third batch hooked us. Within a week, half the neighborhood was stuffed into our little tree house, whipping up slime. We got fancy with glitter and food coloring. After begging our parents to let us make an Instagram page (they finally gave in because "at least we were doing something creative with our hands"), @TreehouseSlimeFactory was born.

That's how I got to know Ashley. She had just moved to Connecticut from Dallas. We found her roaming our neighborhood with her corgis, Valerie and Allen, and invited them all up to watch us work. It was harder than it might seem to hoist two corgis up into a tree house. Ashley held the camera while Will, Mary Kate, and I made the slime. One time, Ashley thought it would be fun to wear press-on nails, since we were modeling our hands. The nails fell off and ended up embedded in the slime.

My granny gave me a really cool plastic case with a secret compartment so I could store my best slimes in Play-Doh containers. I took them out and played with them all the time.

And then one day, we stopped. I don't know when or why. I just got kind of tired of slime. Will was the last one to give it up. I kept the case in my closet for when I was bored and wanted to do some squishing.

Last year, Danny came into my room after he was suspended for the third or fourth time. His teacher caught him vaping during history when they were watching the movie *Glory*.

"You don't still want to keep all that slime in the Play-Doh containers, right?"

I wasn't sure if I did or didn't at that point. "I don't know. Why is it your business?" Danny never, ever talked to me except to make fun of me, yell at me, ask for food, or tell me to go away.

"I want to use the case for my stuff."

"What stuff?"

"My vaping stuff. Mom and Dad are acting like it's a big issue. I don't know what their problem is. It's so much healthier than cigarettes."

I knew it wasn't healthier. I read all the articles Mom left around the house even if Danny didn't. "What do I get?"

"How about I don't punch you?"

"How about you do whatever I say and stop being mean to me and you can have the Play-Doh containers?"

"Fine."

Danny comes into my room all the time now, to get stuff out of the case. Sometimes he talks to me about random things, like concerts coming up and whether or not I would be willing to move to Canada if he had custody of me in the event Mom and Dad die.

It's better than it was before I started renting out the Play-Doh containers.

MY FOUNTAIN BROTHER

My fountain brother is the brother I wish for every time I make a wish in the fountain in front of the Cheesecake Factory.

"Why are you standing there with your eyes closed?" Danny always says. "You look stupid." But I don't care how I look, because with my eyes shut tight I can picture the brother I wish I had.

My fountain brother talks to me when we walk down the street, and asks me if I want ice cream when he gets himself some. He tells me jokes until we collapse in a heap from laughing so hard, and tiptoes with me into Mom and Dad's room with a tray of breakfast food we cooked together (like I see in commercials). My fountain brother protects me when a bunch of boys his age pelt me with ice balls behind the library. He patiently helps me with my homework, instead of saying "How do you not get that?" He reads books with me in blanket forts and never hits me or kicks me or spits into my ear when I'm sleeping or sprays me with the hose when I am all dressed up for my father-daughter Girl Scout dance.

Once, when I was nine or ten, I dumped a mason jar full of money into the fountain, dollar bills and all.

"Why did you do that?" Granny said, fishing out the soggy money. Granny always takes me to the Cheesecake Factory when she visits.

"Please leave the money there," I said. "My wish hasn't come true yet."

Until now, the biggest group chat I've ever been on was sixty people. It was the Scott Kleinman Bar Mitzvah group chat, and it wasn't that exciting, because his mom started it to make sure we all knew when to be at the synagogue, and that we had to cover our shoulders during the service, and that the bus home from the Basketball Hall of Fame would drop us in front of Stop & Shop between eleven and eleven thirty.

That group chat was 90 percent girls asking what people were wearing, until the day before the bar mitzvah. Then it was 90 percent boys asking what people were wearing. One kid kept asking people how much they were giving Scott, because he heard it had to be in multiples of thirteen. Everyone kept texting 18, as in multiples of eighteen. I don't think the kid ever realized Scott *and* his mom could see the whole conversation.

I didn't even know a 217-person group chat was possible until yesterday, when Scott Kleinman (ironically) started a Camping Trip Anyway group chat: **My parents and Jessie Lahey's parents say they'll chaperone if we want to do our own trip to Strawberry Hill. Same day. Reply if you're in.**

Two hundred seventeen of 220 of us are in. I know two kids are heading to India before the end of the year, so they're out. That leaves one eighth-grade classmate unaccounted for.

The parents are having a meeting at the library to discuss the camping trip, because obviously four parents cannot control 217 middle schoolers. I'm praying my parents don't get roped into this. My mom was a room mom five times, and my dad was the DJ at the father-daughter Girl Scout dance. I'll remind them they've done their duty and they should let somebody else step up.

People are cursing a lot in the Camping Trip Anyway group chat.

Nick and his friends are plotting how to smuggle their vape pods. They ask if any of the girls would like to hide pods in their bras. Nobody is answering them.

I kind of hope Scott's mom is reading this one too.

LETTER TO SCOTT KLEINMAN

If it weren't weird to write a letter to Scott Kleinman about his bar mitzvah, I would say this:

Dear Scott,

It looked like you put a lot of work into preparing for your bar mitzvah. It was very brave of you to stand in front of your family and friends and people from out of town (I think your dad said there were people there from California and Miami). You didn't even make a face when the kids from our class wouldn't shut up. I was really impressed with your Hebrew skills and the project you did to educate people about service dogs.

But most of all, I remember the speech your parents gave, about how you have been kind and generous your whole life, including the time you offered your hot pretzel to a girl who had dropped hers (when you were three!). Your parents were so emotional and full of love, and you didn't even seem embarrassed when they hugged you.

I left your bar mitzvah with an empty feeling, because I knew my parents would never be able to give

such a beautiful speech about Danny, and I wasn't
sure they would be able to think of anything special to
say about me.

 Anyway, good job.

 Your classmate,
 Molly

SOMETIMES APPLES ARE JUST EVIL

I used to come home from school and immediately tell my parents all the things Nick and his friends said:

"Nick called Bea 'Pencil Legs.'"

"Nick called Amar 'Isis.'"

"Nick called Liza 'Rice and Beans.'"

"Nick called Scott 'Jew Fro.'"

"Nick spit on Julissa and called her the n-word."

"Nick called Sarah Sims 'a hairy beast man.'"

"Nick called Ashley 'Filet-O-Fish Breath.'"

"Nick called Jacob and another kid with autism 'mental midgets.'"

Even when he said the most horrible things—things that would get Danny and me punished for all eternity—my parents always said, "Just ignore him, Molly. I'm sure he's getting it from somewhere. The apple usually doesn't fall far from the tree."

But I've met Nick's parents. They are really nice. Maybe they are cruel and awful at home, but they were friendly and helpful to everyone when they chaperoned our class morning hikes.

Maybe, just maybe, apples are born evil.

Maybe the tree doesn't have anything to do with it.

Now Nick has all his minions calling Olivia "Tampon

Fail." Nobody ever said his nicknames were clever. I'm sure my parents would tell Olivia to ignore them. He's nothing but an apple rotting on the ground.

I will tell Olivia to fight back, because that's the kind of mood I'm in these days.

DRESS CODED: A PODCAST

ME: My name is Molly Frost, and this is *Dress Coded: A Podcast*. I've decided to speak out on the issue of school dress coding after my friend was humiliated by the principal of our middle school for wearing a tank top that exposed her shoulders. In my opinion, it is wrong to do this to a thirteen-year-old girl. I have invited guests to talk about the issue of dress coding in middle school. Today, I welcome Liza R., who is well known for her volleyball and writing skills. She once wrote a ten-page epic poem about Puerto Rico. It was seriously epic. What was the title, Liza?

LIZA: "Isla Green and Blue."

ME: That's right. It was so good. Okay, so we're here to talk about dress coding. What has been your experience?

LIZA: I had to bring my journal for this one.

ME: Listeners, Liza has opened her journal to the back page, where there are, let me count, five, ten . . . thirty-seven check marks.

LIZA: I started writing it down after that first-day-of-school thing that happened. I stopped wearing the shorts you and I bought together, but no matter what I wore, Fingertip found something wrong. My bra strap was showing, my shirt wasn't long enough, my pants were too tight, my shirt was too low. Her favorite hobby is looking me up and down and finding something wrong with me. No joke.

ME: How does that make you feel?

LIZA: One time, I had a spider in my bathroom sink. I got my brother's magnifying glass and followed the spider all over the place. It was fascinating. Eventually, my mom came in and squished it with the magnifying glass, and I felt really bad for it. How does it make me feel? It makes me feel like that spider.

ME: Wow, Liza.

LIZA: Yeah.

ME: How did things change when they decided to bribe us with the camping trip this year?

LIZA: My mom had to go to Target and spend an entire paycheck on ugly clothes two sizes too big for me, like what I'm wearing right now.

ME: That's not your best look.

LIZA: Right? I know.

ME: Liza, would you like to violate the dress code with me, now that we have nothing to lose?

LIZA: Yes. That would be delightful.

HOW DOES THAT MAKE YOU FEEL?

I learned how to interview people for my podcast by going to therapy. I went to four or five sessions the summer after I quit Lunch Bunch. My mom thought it would be a good idea when she noticed Danny was getting meaner and meaner and I was getting quieter and quieter. The lady (I can't remember her name) always asked me, "How does that make you feel?" And I would always say my dad's favorite word, "Lousy."

Mom told everyone therapy had been a miracle and after only a few sessions I was back to my old self, even though Danny was still being awful.

I was back to my old self because of Treehouse Slime Factory, but the therapy lady helped a little too.

OH, THE PLACES I WON'T GO!

If I sit on the toilet in the half bath near the garage, I can hear everything Mom and Dad say when they're in the den with the door closed. At first, I wasn't trying to listen; I was just sitting on the toilet. But then I heard the word *passport*, and I got curious. Mom tells Dad about the places she wants to move us to so Danny can have a "fresh start." Every time she brings up a place, Dad says, "Well, do some research. I'd be willing to consider it." And Mom says, "We need to be researching this together. It's a big decision." Then they start arguing, and I flush and run.

Here's the list (in no particular order):

Thailand
Scotland
Oregon
Toronto
Florida
Seattle
Portugal
New Zealand

I won't go. I. Won't. Go.

Liza and I are both going to wear normal-length shorts. We make a plan while our moms talk out in the driveway.

Liza says, "I'll wear the outfit, but it seems like we could do something bigger than the two of us getting ourselves dress coded and refusing to change our clothes."

"Okay, like what?"

"Let me think about it."

"Let's just wear the outfits tomorrow and see what happens," I say.

In the morning, I almost remind my mom that she agreed not to be mad if I got dress coded, but I decide against it. I don't want to give her a chance to take it back. She doesn't even notice I'm wearing the shorts, and I wear a hoodie over the tank top. When I get to school, the hoodie goes into my locker.

It feels like the first day of seventh grade, when I ran around lost and scared Fingertip would send me to the office. Liza must be feeling the same way. I sit down in homeroom without any issues, probably because Ms. Lane is one of my favorite teachers ever. She would never shame people for wearing a tank top and shorts.

My legs are sticking to the cold seat. I look down and notice a pretty obvious shaving rash on my upper thighs.

These rashes have become a big problem for me. I need to see my dermatologist. First, it was acne, now shaving rashes. What's next?

Liza comes running over during lunch. I'm at the usual lunch table, with Bea, Ashley, Navya, and a kid named Tom who has a traumatic brain injury from a skiing accident and is kind of confused a lot of the time. We're the only ones who pay attention to him.

"Maybe you should ask Tom to the prom," my mom has said at least twice, because she has POD—prom obsessive disorder. It will likely get worse between now and three years from now, when I actually need to think about prom.

"Did you get dress coded?" Liza asks, sitting down across from Tom.

"Not yet," I say. "Did you?"

"Uh. Yes. Fingertip pulled me out of the line for library books and told me my shorts were too short. I told her my mom would sue her for harassment if she bugged me about it again."

"No, you did not," Ashley says.

"Okay, I didn't. But I wanted to. I just said my mom is a nurse and she can't leave the hospital to get me clothes. She asked me where my dad was, and I said taking care of my sick aunt in Puerto Rico. She told me this was a warning, and if I don't knock it off, she'll call my parents in for a meeting and she doesn't care how far away they are."

"That's so rude," Navya says.

"Hey, Tom," Bea says. "Do Liza's shorts distract you from your schoolwork?"

Tom looks at Liza's shorts. "As in why?" he asks.

"Never mind. Dumb question."

I spend the rest of the day doing the exact opposite of the first day of seventh grade. I try to get the teachers to dress code me. Nobody does.

Dern sees me and turns to talk to one of the baseball players.

Is it because Liza has boobs and a butt and long legs? Is that why he sees her and ignores me?

Is that why I'm invisible?

THE PARENT MEETING AT THE LIBRARY TAKES A TURN

My mom walks in from the meeting at the library about the camping trip, throws her keys on the counter, and runs up the stairs. I'm assuming she's excited to tell me she volunteered to chaperone.

"Hi, Molly," she says, sitting down on the bed, where all my science notes are scattered on the butter-yellow comforter. "The meeting was interesting."

"Oh yeah. Did parents fight over whether or not to have whole-wheat graham crackers for s'mores, like they did at the jamboree last year?"

She laughs. It's a very strained laugh. "No. And I should tell you I didn't volunteer to be a chaperone. I would have if they didn't have enough people, but you know, I'd like to be here with Danny."

"I get it."

"Honey, why didn't you tell me? That's terrible. People are really upset that Olivia was treated like that."

"It's pretty standard at that school."

"Molly, I had no idea."

"Mom, you knew about the dress code and you knew they bribed us with the camping trip."

"Dr. Couchman is definitely a follow-the-rules kind of guy, but this is way out of line."

"I'm working on a podcast. I'm interviewing people about their embarrassing dress-code experiences."

"You are, Molly?"

"Yeah. It really bothers me."

"You wear whatever you want to school, okay? And if anyone gives you a problem, you tell me."

"Thanks, Mom."

"You know, maybe you and your classmates could start a petition asking to have the dress code removed from the handbook."

"Where would we send it? Dr. Couchman would laugh and toss it in the trash. He'll never give up his laminated dress-code page. It's like his designer purse. He carries it everywhere."

"You can send it to the superintendent, or the interim superintendent, I guess they're calling him. It's worth a try."

"Okay. I guess it's worth a try."

She gives me a look that says *I'm proud of you*, and I get a pang of guilt in my stomach for hiding Danny's stuff. I get that pang about five times a day, and I wonder if Danny is worth it.

MOTHER'S DAY

I give my mom a silver ladybug charm because she loves ladybugs. I design a ladybug card, like I do every year, and tell her she's the best mom in the world. Dad and I make blueberry pancakes with homemade whipped cream and bring them on a tray with mint tea and a vase full of fresh-picked lilacs to Mom on the back deck. She cries when she reads my card, like hard-cries, not the usual tiny *aww* cry. She says she wants to sit on the back deck all day and drink in the sunshine and read her book.

I visit her in between cleaning the house and folding laundry.

Danny doesn't even remember it's Mother's Day, or if he does, he doesn't mention it.

Last Mother's Day, Danny stole the extra set of car keys from the cabinet next to the cookie-cutter drawer, and he tried to drive away in Mom's car, even though he doesn't have a driver's license. Mom ran up the street screaming, and Will's dad chased him with his truck and cut him off, and Danny hit the side of the truck. Everyone was okay, but Mom hyperventilated on Mary Kate's front lawn.

That night, she told Dad he had to stop DJ'ing on the weekends, which he loved, because she couldn't do this alone. She couldn't do Danny alone. Dad's last gig was a Mother's Day garden party. His last song was "Tiny Dancer" by Elton John, the song he played for me all the time when I was little.

That's why they're always worrying about money.

That's why Mom cried when she read my card.

That's why they talk about moving our whole family to another country.

That's why I tried so hard to make Mom happy today.

Other than Nick calling Olivia "Tampon Fail," most people have forgiven Olivia for ruining the trip, especially since we're going on the trip anyway.

Ashley is furious her dad volunteered to chaperone, and that he wants to bring his fishing equipment. "How are we supposed to sneak out now?" she says. "My dad will be sitting in front of our tent with a fishing rod and gross bait worms." We're at lunch, eating ice cream bars and chips, as usual.

"You could rub poison ivy on your dad," Tom says.

Ashley looks at Tom. "That's actually not a bad idea."

Navya runs over with the petition we wrote during study hall. She made copies in Ms. Lane's room.

PETITION TO REMOVE THE DRESS CODE
FROM THE STUDENT HANDBOOK AND
ALLOW STUDENTS TO DRESS AS THEY CHOOSE

"Who's going to sign first?" Navya asks.

"I will," I say.

We pass it around the hallways, the locker room, the bathroom, and the school buses. By four o'clock, all one hundred slots are filled, and we need more pages.

We get nearly every girl and a lot of boys in the seventh and eighth grades to sign, and Mom drives me to the interim superintendent's office to hand-deliver the 312 signatures to his secretary.

Now we wait.

WEEKLY BULLETIN

- Remember to check the lost-and-found table. It's overflowing!
- Be bear aware! We've had two Code Browns this month.
- Reminder: Moving Up Day attire is white dresses for girls and dress pants, dress shirts, and ties for boys.

Have a great week and enjoy the sunshine!

—Mrs. Peabody

MOST TRIPS TO THE MALL INVOLVE PRETZELS

Our eighth-grade graduation is still weeks away, but Ashley wants to go dress shopping after school so she can claim the best dress, post it on Instagram, and make sure nobody else buys it. Mom says I can go looking, and she gives me seventy-five dollars for a dress, in case I find one.

We've never been the wealthiest people in town, but since Mom stopped working and Dad stopped DJ'ing, we don't go out to dinner, we don't plan trips, and we don't buy expensive clothes that we're only going to wear once.

Now I get what *tight budget* means.

Ashley's mom has to return things at Lord & Taylor, so Ashley and I go straight to Nordstrom. Somebody said there were a lot of white dresses there.

White dresses. Why? It's not a First Communion. We're not being baptized. It's not a *wedding*.

We check Snap Map. Great. Nick is here with his squad. I don't want to run into them, because they'll make fun of my greasy hair and because Ashley kind of flirts with all of them and it's a disgusting spectacle. Her energy has changed from carefree dress shopper to twitchy squirrel girl.

We make it to the Nordstrom juniors' dress section, and Ashley immediately sees a dress. It's off-white but really pretty, with crisscross straps and pearls stitched onto the neckline. I look around and realize I will probably need to go to the kids' section, because I'm still technically a 12–14. She comes out looking ravishing, like seriously she could get married in this dress if it weren't short and she weren't thirteen. She poses for twenty pictures while she waits for her mom.

The comments start coming in: **Hot. Lit. Super cute.**

"Oh, Ash, that's perfect. Wow. Done!" her mom says. "Let's get shoes and we can cross this off our to-do list. Score!"

"That's a weird thing to say, Mom," Ashley says, turning to go to the dressing room.

"Any luck, Molly?" her mom asks.

"I'm kind of not in the mood to try on dresses. I'm sweaty."

"Oh, I know that feeling. Sweaty and bloated are deal breakers for me."

We make our way down to the shoe department, and Ashley's mom grabs five pairs of high-heel shoes. The shoe guy comes out with a stack of boxes, and Ashley tries on pair after pair.

She likes the highest ones, of course. And her mom says, "Your feet are going to be screaming by the end of the night."

"That's so weird, Mom."

I stand at the counter while Ashley's mom pays $372. That's the total.

Ashley has a huge house, and her dad drives a Lexus, and her mom wears a giant diamond ring. I know those facts. But when I see the way her mom doesn't even look at the amount when she swipes her platinum-colored credit card, I understand all too clearly that Ashley is rich and I am not and I am going to need to find a dress for seventy-five dollars (one that goes with the shoes I've worn to every bar and bat mitzvah for the past two years).

We're walking toward the exit, and something bounces off my head and lands on the floor in front of me. I reach up and cover my face just as I'm hit again in the shoulder.

Ashley runs ahead and yells at the balcony above, "Nick, knock it off." She's sort of laughing. Nick is throwing pretzel bites at me, and Ashley thinks it's funny.

I feel myself turning red inside.

I dart into Pink and wait for Ashley to find me. I'm in no mood to deal with Nick and his friends. They probably wander around the mall every day staring at Snap Map until they find familiar faces to pelt with pretzel bites.

I look both ways and drag Ashley to Auntie Anne's, because now I want pretzels. I spend seven dollars on a pretzel with dipping sauce and a lemonade. That leaves sixty-eight dollars for my white dress. We sit on the edge of the fountain and eat while Ashley posts pictures of herself.

It's true that I'm pretty sweaty. But I don't feel like looking for dresses because lurking Nick and being not rich are deal breakers for me.

DRESS CODED: A PODCAST

ME: Hello, Fisher Middle School and beyond. My name is Molly Frost, and this is *Dress Coded: A Podcast*. Today, I'm interviewing Pearl P., tennis player, leader of the FMS community service club, eighth-grade editor of our school's literary magazine, and founder of the Pan-Asian Alliance. Am I missing anything?

PEARL: No. That's about it.

ME: So can you tell me about your experiences with dress coding at Fisher?

PEARL: Well, I've never actually been dress coded. But I've watched my friends being pulled over too many times. And I saw the incident in the garden. It upset me so much I wrote a poem about it that night.

ME: Oh. Can you share the poem?

PEARL: Maybe someday. Anyway, I watched our principal and another teacher yelling at my friend, who was humiliated and crying, and it made me so mad. And yet I didn't know what to do to help her. I just stood there. I was frozen.

ME: I know. Me too. How did that make you feel?

PEARL: Like a fly caught in a spiderweb watching another fly get devoured by two gross hairy spiders.

This is the third Fisher Middle School girl in a week who has compared herself to a bug.

PEARL: And I think about all the girls in my little sister's class who are running around just happy being kids. I don't want them to have to go through this.

ME: Do you ever wonder why you were never dress coded?

PEARL: No. I don't need to wonder.

She points to her chest.

PEARL: I wear the same clothes from the same stores as Liza and Bea and everyone else. I'm just, you know.

ME: Smaller.

PEARL: Smaller.

And at Fisher Middle School, smaller means invisible.

PEARL: Did you know Catherine, the girl who transferred to Catholic school, got dress coded last year because she had a fever? Her face was red, and she was leaning on the wall, saying she felt dizzy. They had the heat cranked up, and she took off her hoodie because she was so hot. Couchman swooped in and made her put her hoodie on because her shoulders were showing. He didn't look at her face. If he had, he would have seen she was obviously really sick. She was out two weeks. He probably didn't even notice.

ME: Do you think Couchman ever looks at anyone's face?

PEARL: He's never looked at mine.

A CAIRN IS A PILE OF STONES

I walk Pearl through the woods behind my house. It's warm, and the air is thick with pollen, the kind that looks like mustard and sticks to the surfaces of lawn chairs and car hoods. We carry a broom just in case we run into bears— yes, bears. They call our town ground zero for bears in Connecticut. They're usually shy, but mother bears with cubs don't mess around.

Pearl's mom is late picking her up in front of the Fisher tennis courts, so we walk over to the FMS garden. Mrs. Tucker's pile of kindness rocks is a cairn, a makeshift memorial to the death of childhood.

Every year, on the first day of school, Mrs. Tucker wears a necklace made of tiny kindness rocks. She gathers the seventh graders in the gym and asks them to return the next day with a special rock and a word or phrase that they will carry with them through middle school.

I was so excited that morning, with my new outfit and my backpack with tons of pockets and a glittery M key chain. I couldn't wait to find my rock and think of the perfect word or phrase. An hour later, I heard about Liza getting in trouble and spent the rest of my first day hiding from teachers. I forgot to bring in the rock the next day, and Mrs. Tucker had to give me one from her reject rock box. I painted it blue and got stuck trying to find the perfect word. I ended up copying Bea, who painted *Be Kind* on both sides.

Be Kind. What an unoriginal thing to write on a kindness rock. Other than Nick and his friends and a couple of girls who are more bossy than unkind, I don't know many kids who are deliberately mean. Most of them are so focused on being popular or getting good grades or disappearing into the crowd, they forget to think of anyone else. But they don't *try* to be unkind. I should have written *Be Kind* on one side and *To Yourself* on the other, and then remembered to say it five times a day.

"What did you write on your rock?" I ask Pearl. She's taking a picture of a butterfly perched on the top of a rosebush.

She laughs. " 'Choose Kindness.' "

"Wow. That's as original as 'Be Kind.' "

"What would you write now?" Pearl asks.

I pause. "Probably 'Choose Homeschooling.' "

Pearl's mom pulls up. Her sister jumps out of the car and runs into the garden. "Look at the butterfly," Pearl says. Her sister's little, maybe five or six, and so happy to run up and down the rows of flowers.

Carefree.

Shame-free.

Free.

LETTER TO MY FIRST-GRADE DAISY TROOP

If I could write a letter to my first-grade Daisy troop, I would glue it to a piece of cardboard and decorate it with pasta shapes dipped in glitter paint. That would get their attention.

Dear Daisies,

I know you are excited to go on the trip to the Bronx Zoo and earn a badge (I can't remember which one it is). Soon, you will pack lunches and Emma will invite us over to paint our faces with animal designs before we meet at the bus. We already chose our bus seat partners. I'm sitting with you, Bea.

Emma won't invite Megan Birch to do the face painting. Megan will show up at the bus smiling and excited, just like the rest of us. But her face will drop when she sees twelve faces painted like tigers and birds and butterflies.

Megan's face will drop again when twelve of us board the bus and scramble to our seats in pairs, and she sits all by herself.

How do you think Megan will feel, Daisies?
How would you feel?

Megan Birch is smart and funny, and she loves horses and graphic novels. I know this because she was my lab partner this year in eighth grade. She walks and talks that way because she has CP, short for cerebral palsy. It's not her fault.

That's how she was born.

You will run around the zoo, checking off animals on your worksheet and laughing at all the different sizes and shapes of animal poop. Before boob *is the funniest word you know,* poop *will stay funny for a very long time.*

Megan will lag behind, not because of the way she walks, but because we will have sucked out pieces of her soul. It happens that way, Daisies. Trust me.

It is possible to be cruel by exclusion. (I don't know if you know those words yet. I don't remember what words kids know in first grade.) But we will be cruel by exclusion, and Megan Birch will be alone most of her childhood.

It doesn't take much to be kind.

WHEN YOUR BEST FRIEND IS A BOY, SOMETIMES CONVERSATIONS WILL BE AWKWARD

I run into Will on my way back through the woods. He's sitting at the picnic table, trying to get his dad's drone to work.

"What are you doing with the drone?" I say.

"I want to see if the lacrosse game is still going on."

"Why don't you just check Snap?"

"I got my phone taken away."

"That game?"

"Yup."

"Hey, I'm still mad at you for what you said about Olivia."

He shakes his head. "How was I supposed to know she had a tampon fail?"

"Do you even know what a tampon fail is?"

"Not completely. What is it?"

I change the subject. "Do you think the dress code is ridiculous? Honestly?"

He takes the drone apart and sets the pieces on the table. "I can tell you I'm glad I'm not a girl. I wouldn't want to be accused of ruining the camping trip."

"Do shoulders distract boys?"

He laughs. "Give me a break, Molly."

"How about legs?"

"Do you think two inches of fabric makes a difference with boys? It's not going to determine whether I can concentrate in math class or not. Give boys a little credit. We're not wild animals."

"Some of you are."

"Yeah. I guarantee that has nothing to do with what girls wear."

"Would you be willing to say that on a podcast?"

"What? Why?"

"I'm doing a podcast series on dress coding at Fisher."

"Yeah. I'm sure that wouldn't get me pushed into a locker."

"Oh, come on. Nobody actually pushes people into lockers. Be brave."

"Come with me to gym sometime."

Will convinces me to stay and fly the drone with him. It's loud, and I'm sure it's waking up every napping baby in the neighborhood. I put on the goggles and fly over Fisher Middle School and the soccer fields, the gas station and the nature preserve, Starbucks, the pizza place, the other pizza place, and the Thai restaurant. I soar over the high school and try not to think about the fact that I'll be in there soon, trying to find my way. Will slows the drone over the lacrosse field.

"Game's over," I say.

"I didn't feel like going anyway," he says. "Is Danny home?"

I pull the goggles off and glare at him. "You better not be vaping."

"Never, Molly. You know me."

I do know Will. "You're not coming over for your gaming fix."

"How about if I agree to do your podcast?"

"I'll think about it."

CONTACT INFORMATION

Navya and I gave our emails and phone numbers as contacts for the interim superintendent. We check our emails and phone messages every day. And every day, no response.

WHITE DRESSES GROUP CHAT

Bea started the White Dresses group chat after Ashley posted pictures of her dress. Mom let me order four from Lulus if I promised to go into the post office to return the rejects. (Mom hates the post office.)

Bea adds most of the girls in our class to the group chat.

I add my lab partner, Megan Birch.

I check to see if Megan Birch is the one kid missing from our class-trip yes list and discover she's on the list. It's not her.

I'm freezing. I knew it would be cold and rainy, but I wanted to wear shorts anyway, because I'm determined to get dress coded before the end of middle school. It didn't happen today (as usual). I snuggle up next to Mary Kate in the front seat of the bus and start to organize my binder. I have four tests tomorrow.

"Are you Molly?" I look around for the source of the voice. A senior is standing up in the seat behind us, staring down at me.

"Yeah." I'm scared. She's old, like the oldest person on the bus not counting the driver. I have no idea how a senior would know my name.

"I heard your podcast about the body shaming."

"You did?"

The podcast went live last night at midnight. Bea uploaded episodes one and two, and we shared it all over the place. So far, the only person who mentioned it was this girl named Delia who has insomnia. Her feedback was pretty positive.

"Yeah. I want to tell you what happened to me and my friends when we were at the middle school. It was messed up," the senior says.

I look into her eyes and feel the boldness grow inside me.

"Would you be willing to be interviewed for the podcast?"

She hesitates. "Yes. I'll definitely do the podcast."

I don't know how I'm going to fit a senior in my tree house.

CHERRY PIE

I don't know if I would have survived science this year without Megan Birch. Some people get it. Some people don't. She gets it. I don't. We're sitting on our stools at the tall table in the back of the room, waiting for the teacher to go find some mystery thing he forgot in the teachers' lounge.

Megan and I FaceTimed last night for about three hours. That's how long it took her to explain tectonic plates to me. Well, it didn't actually take the whole three hours. Part of that time was spent giving each other tours of our rooms. Megan's room is lemon yellow, and her walls are covered with Polaroid pictures of her and her best friend, this kid Graham, who used to go to our school, but transferred to Catholic in seventh grade.

Seeing Megan's room made me want to redo my room completely. But that won't happen until I get a job, unless somebody dies and leaves me money.

Megan reaches into her backpack and pulls out two Hershey's Kisses.

"Want one?" she asks.

I take it, peel off the green foil, and pop it into my mouth. "Thanks. Are these the Christmas ones?"

She laughs. "Yeah. I keep them in the freezer for"—she hesitates—"you know, that time of the month."

Normally I would nod in agreement and lie and say I also have a freezer full of chocolate for my time of the month, but Megan is like a human truth serum. For some reason, she makes me want to tell her the truth.

I lean over and whisper in her ear, "I don't have mine yet." She smells like Bea. I think they use the same shampoo.

She nods. "Lucky. Look at this." She points to the tiny pimples dotting her forehead and nose. "It's like a topographical map." I'm guessing she doesn't talk about this stuff with Graham.

"Oh, I get those. Mine are big crusty ones." I feel around the side of my nose. "This is like that one big volcano in the middle of a quiet island."

"You're going to get it soon. Be ready."

"Don't worry. I have the embroidered maxi-pad pouch my granny made me." I pat the front pocket of my backpack.

"Aww. That's sweet."

Mr. Lu kicks the door open and walks in carrying an enormous pie.

"Whoa. Is it your birthday?" Tom yells out.

"Nope. It's your test." He sets the pie on the front table, takes out a cake knife, and slices into it.

"Are you allowed to have a knife in school?" Jack Reese asks. Mr. Lu gives him a weird look and keeps cutting.

He lays a giant slice on a paper plate and points to the middle of the pie. "This, friends, is a cross section of your planet. There are three layers: the streusel topping, the cherry filling, and the graham cracker crust. Label them and write an essay about them, and when you're finished, we'll eat."

"I'm allergic to all stone fruits," this girl named Amelia says.

"I don't get this," Jack says.

Mr. Lu was trying to be cute and clever, but nobody understands the pie test assignment, and Mr. Lu ends up saying, "Forget it." He pulls a file folder off his desk and hands out regular tests.

Earth's crust.

Pie crust.

Pimple crust.

They're all connected if you think about it long enough.

o o o

Will runs up to me after school and asks if he can borrow my phone to call his mom and tell her he's not staying late for Robotics Club and ask if she can pick him up and take him to get pizza.

"How long is your phone gone?" I ask when she doesn't answer and he and I decide to walk home through the woods.

"Until the end of the summer."

I stop dead. "What? They took it away for four months because you played that game too much? That's it?"

He hesitates. "They think I'm addicted."

"You're totally addicted, but that's a cruel and unusual punishment."

We pause so Will can tie his shoe.

"My mom freaked out when she came into my room and I was sick but I didn't stop playing."

"Why did she freak out?"

"Well, I kind of had the stomach bug, and I sort of puked in the garbage can next to my bed because I didn't feel like going to the bathroom since I was playing the game."

I take a few steps away from him. "Oh, gross, Will. You are disgusting."

"Thank you. My mom made that pretty clear."

"Are you actually going to quit?"

He shrugs. "I might."

We cut through his yard and head for the tree house. "Are you going to do the podcast?" I ask, almost forgetting the senior is coming over tomorrow night.

"I don't really have anything to say about the dress code."

"Lucky you."

I run into the house and grab two bags of chips and a glass of seltzer to share. I get halfway to the tree house and run back for another glass, remembering Will just had the stomach bug. When I get up there, Will is in his spot, lying on his back, with his head on my Winnie-the-Pooh pillow and his feet planted on the wall.

"Did you guys get pie in science today?" I ask, suddenly realizing why I'm not as hungry as I usually am after school.

"No, why?"

I'm guessing Mr. Lu decided eighth graders weren't worth good pie. He's probably out in his car in the parking lot eating Will's class's pie with a plastic spork.

"How well do you know that girl Pearl?" Will asks, out of the blue.

He never asks me about girls.

"Why? Do you like her?"

His face goes cherry-pie red, and I'm not sure how I feel about this.

"Pretty well," I say, and then I realize something. "Is that why you're up here? Are you hoping she shows up?"

"Molly, I've spent eighty percent of my life up here."

"And eight percent of eighth grade. Do the math." I take a sip of seltzer. "I don't care, Will. Just be honest."

"I'm leaving. You're annoying."

"Go puke on your video game."

BEFORE THE TREE HOUSE WAS A RECORDING STUDIO FOR PODCASTS, IT WAS:[1]

1. A grotto for mermaids and mermen. Piles of sea-shells. Buckets of sand from our old sand table. Fabric in shades of blue hanging everywhere.
2. A fairy house. Shimmer fabric in shades of pink, yellow, and green. Tissue-paper flowers. Cutout butterflies with huge googly eyes.
3. The boxcar from the Boxcar Children books. Spoons, tin plates, a knapsack, crackers, and plain cookies. Red-and-white-checked fabric for the windows.
4. A keep. Cardboard swords wrapped in foil. Many, many of them.
5. The Gryffindor common room. Red and gold, with wands made out of repurposed foil swords.

The floorboards don't fit perfectly together. There are gaps, like gaps between teeth before braces. It's all stuck in the gaps—bits of fabric, sand, glitter, foil, red and gold, tiny seashells, probably a thousand cookie crumbs.

And magic.

There's a lot of magic in that floor.

---

1. Decorations courtesy of Michaels, where my mom took us every time we had an idea.

DRESS CODED: A PODCAST

ME: Hello, Fisher Middle School and beyond. My name is Molly Frost, and this is *Dress Coded: A Podcast*, episode four. Today, I'm interviewing senior in high school Jessica H. about her experience at Fisher Middle. Thank you for agreeing to do this, Jessica.

She brought her friend Jasmine. The friend is sitting in the corner, staring at us and eating an energy bar. But she seems nice, and much less scary than I had originally thought.

JESSICA: Sure. No problem. I haven't told many people about what happened to us, so I'm glad you started this.

ME: *[Clears throat.]* We usually say a few things about the guest. Do you want to tell us anything about yourself before you share your story?

JESSICA: Um, I got into Vanderbilt early decision, so I'm pretty excited about that. And I'm seventeen school days away from being done with this place.

ME: Wait, I thought it was eighteen.

JESSICA: Senior Skip Day. We have one day less than you.

ME: Oh yeah.

JESSICA: Do you want me to just start?

ME: Sure. So tell me what it was like back when you were at Fisher Middle School. Did you have the same dress-code policy?

JESSICA: Yeah. It was not good. Actually, Couchman started there when we were in seventh grade. The principal before him, Ms. Milholland, hadn't paid attention to the student handbook. She took the Math Olympian team to nationals. Do they still have that?

ME: Yes. Only like three kids do it, and one is a fifth grader who skipped grades.

JESSICA: Ms. Milholland was a legend. My mom had her as a teacher before she became principal. Everyone loved her.

ME: I've heard so many good things about her.

JESSICA: My sister never got dress coded once, and believe me, she would have had a target on her back if Couchman were there. When he started, he followed the student handbook like it was the United States Constitution. Not even—the Constitution is open to interpretation. He followed it like it was some sort of fascism manual.

ME: Did he start dress coding right away?

JESSICA: The first day of school, a bunch of my friends got pulled over in the hall and told to read the handbook and follow it or they'd be in trouble. After that, he hired Fingertip to patrol the school in search of bare shoulders and leg skin and bra straps, and whatever else he was looking for. Then one day—I still remember the date, September fourteenth, because it was my friend Vani's birthday and I was bent over with my head in my locker trying to find the gift I got her—I felt someone tap me on my lower back, and figured it was one of the obnoxious boys. But it was Couchman standing over me. He told me to follow him. I was really nervous and scared I would get in trouble for being late to my first math quiz with cranky Mr. Dern.

ME: Oh, yes. He's still cranky.

JESSICA: So he led me to the library, where four other girls were sitting at a table. I knew one of them and kind of knew the others. I had no idea why we were there. But then he closed the door behind us and made us line up in front of the windows. He told us to look at each other, because we were all in violation of the dress code, and if we violated it again we would have to go home and change, and if we kept doing it we would be suspended. One girl, who now happens to be one of my best friends, was kind of mouthy. She still is, but whatever, she's going to be a famous attorney someday. Anyway, she asked what was wrong with our outfits. He pulled out a laminated paper and was waving it around. We later found out he had ripped the dress code from the school handbook and laminated it. He said our shorts were to be past our fingertips, and our bra straps couldn't be showing. He actually used the d-word. He said our clothes were a *distraction* to boys who were trying to take school seriously. The girl who is now one of my best friends laughed, and he got really mad and sent her to the office. Her dad had to bring her a shirt that didn't show her bra straps, and he had no idea what shirt to bring, and she got really mad at him for bringing her the ugliest shirt she owned. The whole thing was a big mess.

ME: That's horrible.

JESSICA: The worst part was that while Couchman was so focused on not disturbing the boys' learning with our distracting shoulders, I missed my first math quiz. Dern wouldn't let me make it up, and I got an F. It was the first and only F I ever got.

ME: Wow. Did your parents do anything about it?

JESSICA: My dad called his friend on the school board and said it's an absurd policy and they need to change it. His friend said they'd look into it, but they never did, and my dad forgot about it when I got to the high school.

ME: Did anything change?

JESSICA: If anything, it got worse. Fingertip dress coded all of us a bunch more times. I was always really self-conscious about my stomach, so I'd pull my shirt down to cover my stomach, and she'd dress code me for wearing a "revealing" shirt. Ugh. I was miserable.

ME: It's just so unfair.

JESSICA: There are so many stories.

She looks over at her friend, who is wiping tears from her face.

JESSICA: Hey, what's wrong, honey?

JASMINE: Sorry. Middle school was really bad.

JESSICA: She was dress coded more than me, *and* girls were mean to her, *and* boys were rude. You know, because she's gorgeous.

JASMINE: No, I'm not.

JESSICA: Oh, please. You're stunning. Molly, keep doing this. It's so important. It doesn't have to be like this.

ME: What do you think we should do?

JESSICA: Fight him.

JASMINE: Fight him so girls can finally dress in peace.

ME: Dress in peace. I like that.

The Jessica podcast goes live at midnight.

@DRESSCODEDAPODCAST

We now have an Instagram page. After Jessica's podcast, we got over a hundred followers and a ton of high school people posting pictures of themselves in outfits that got them dress coded at Fisher Middle School.

It's pretty cool.

Today, I posted an update:

As of 4 p.m., we have still not heard from the interim superintendent about our petition to end dress coding at Fisher Middle School. We called his secretary. She said he would be reviewing our petition "soon."

SHRINE TO MS. MILHOLLAND

Our language arts teacher, Ms. Lane, has a shrine to the old principal, Ms. Milholland, on a painted red shelf next to her desk. She tells us we should all seek out mentors and that Ms. Milholland was her mentor. On the shelf, she keeps: a picture of Ms. Milholland addressing the school, her arms reaching up toward the ceiling; a birthday card from Ms. Milholland; a glass bird; a pewter elephant charm; and Ms. Milholland's desk nameplate.

We all thought Ms. Milholland was dead until a few months ago, when she surprised Ms. Lane with the glass bird and a cupcake on her birthday. She was smaller and younger than I thought she'd be after hearing about all the parents she had taught. She's younger than Granny, and as sweet as a cupcake.

She made Ms. Lane cry.

I'll guarantee Ms. Lane is *still* waiting for that "happy birthday" from Dr. Couchman.

HAVE YOU ACTUALLY TRIED
ON A GARBAGE BAG?

Mary Kate tells me all about her science assignment on the bus. She's studying red-tide algae's effect on manatees in Florida, and from the sound of it, it's terrifying.

"I love manatees," I say.

"They're dying, and it's so sad. People are polluting the water, which isn't helping."

I feel like middle school has changed Mary Kate, like she's not the same petrified girl from the first day. She has an edge now.

"Where's Danny?" she asks, handing me a gummy worm.

"No clue. My mom probably picked him up."

I check the mailbox and find a Lulus package shoved in along with a flyer for lawn services and a Bed Bath & Beyond 20-percent-off coupon. Mom and Danny are yelling at each other when I walk in, but I ignore them and run upstairs to try on my dresses. I close the door and tear open the package. The dresses are all really cute. I can't go wrong here.

The first one is too big.

The second one reminds me of my granny's favorite saying, "It fits you like a garbage bag."

The third one also fits like a garbage bag.

Danny stomps up the stairs and slams his door.

I take a deep breath and try on the last one. We got them in the smallest size they had. If this one doesn't fit, I'm back to square one. I stand in front of the mirror and pull number four over my head.

It fits. Like. A. Garbage. Bag.

I carefully fold the dresses and stuff them back into the package. I could text my friends and see if any of them want to try on the dresses before I take them to the post office, but I don't feel like it.

It could be so much worse.

I could be a manatee swimming in a red algae sea.

CARNIVAL COLORS

The Saint Mary's Parish carnival happens every year on the weekend between Mother's Day and Memorial Day. Nobody really goes to the carnival after middle school, so this is it, our last chance to walk around a big field of grubby rides in giant groups, staring at the kids who go to Catholic, while eating snow cones and cotton candy and trying to look pretty.

It's like the mall threw up on my floor. I've pulled every last item of clothing from my closet and drawers, tried them in various combinations, sent pictures of those combinations to my friends, and here I am—hopeless.

"Wear the black leggings and the cropped blue shirt," Navya says when she walks in. "It's fine."

"You look amazing. I don't want to look *fine*."

Navya sits at my desk and turns on the makeup mirror. I'm so frustrated I want to scream. I pull on the leggings and the cropped blue shirt and shove her over. We share a chair and paint our faces carnival colors.

"What's going on with Ashley?" Navya asks.

"Why? What do you mean?"

"She told Bea she thinks the podcasts are annoying and she can't believe we made an Instagram account to complain about the dress code."

I stare at her in the mirror. "What?"

"Yeah. Have you noticed she's always quiet when we're talking about it?"

"Do you think it's her mom?" I ask.

"I think Ashley and her mom are two peas in one pod."

"I'm asking her right now," I say.

"No, don't do that."

> **ME:** Hey, question. Do you want to do the next podcast episode?

No answer.

> **ME:** Ashleyyyyyyy? Are you there?

No answer. And then—

ASHLEY: I don't really care about the dress code. It's annoying, but it's not worth getting all crazy, Molly.

> **ME:** All crazy? What does that mean?

ASHLEY: Nothing. The answer is no, thank you. I'm not interested.

"Wow. I guess she's not interested," I say.

"She's just being Ashley."

ME: Sounds good, Ash. We'll see you at the carnival.

Bea's mom drives us to the parking lot entrance. My heart is beating so hard it's practically bursting through the blue crop top. It's too much—the bright lights, the loud music, the smell of hot sausage, and the faces of literally every kid from my school *and* Catholic all mixed together. I've waited years for the day our parents would leave us here without supervision. And now I don't want to be here at all.

"Come on, let's go find people we know," Bea says, grabbing my hand. "Yuck. Your hand is clammy."

"Leave me alone," I say, wiping my hands on my leggings.

It takes a while to find our rhythm. We meet up with Liza and her cousin from New York, and the lacrosse team and some other random people. I see Pearl and Olivia and wave to Megan Birch, who is riding the Ferris wheel with her best friend, the kid who goes to Catholic.

"Where's Ashley?" Bea asks.

We finally find her in line for popcorn with her neighbor Rachel.

"I thought Ashley hated Rachel," Navya whispers.

"Me too," I say.

We make a bad decision to go on some rides after we eat. It's getting dark, and Bea and I find a bench behind the porta-potties to rest our stomachs. That's when I see my brother surrounded by a pack of seventh graders.

"Why is Danny here?" Bea asks, but she stops herself. "Oh."

"Yeah. Danny knows where to find middle school kids with wads of carnival cash."

I feel gross—from the food, the rides, Ashley, my brother.

All this time, I've been sad that this is the last parish carnival of my life. Now I get why high school kids don't want to come to this thing.

Bea's cute white shorts are filthy.

I'm glad I wore the black leggings.

Danny comes to my room after eleven. He locks my door, goes into the closet, and pulls out the slime case. He opens a couple of Play-Doh containers and drops mango pods into one and crème brûlée pods into the other. Then he puts a pod in his device and breathes in the vapor.

"Can you not do that in my room?" I snap.

"Sorry. My bad." He flings himself on the bed next to me and picks up my phone. "Somebody's trying to talk to you."

I grab the phone. "Okay, can you not touch my stuff, Danny?"

"Do you think I would make a good pilot?" he asks, staring at me.

"I don't know. Do you want to be a pilot?"

"I'm thinking about it. I'm trying to figure out how to get a pilot's license."

"You don't even have your driver's license."

"Yeah, because our parents are the worst."

He fluffs my pillow and rolls over on his side. "No way. You still have Candy Land?" He hangs over the edge of the bed and reaches for the battered Candy Land box under the nightstand.

We once played Candy Land for four and half hours straight.

"One game?" he asks.

"I'm trying to get ready for bed, Danny."

"One game, sister."

"Fine."

We play five games. Then six. I win game seven, and he begs for another, but I fold the board and put our players, Mr. Blue and Miss Yellow, to bed in their box.

"I'm hungry," I say.

"Me too," Danny says. "I want candy."

The phone rings at seven a.m. on the dot. I hear Mom shout, "Steve, come down here now."

I sit on the floor under my open window so I can hear what my parents are saying out on the deck.

"She called the police, and I don't blame her. They're going to get the school involved, because he's been selling on the bus. Oh, I can't breathe."

I run downstairs. Mom is on her hands and knees, trying to catch her breath, while Dad rubs her back.

"Dad, what's wrong?"

He shakes his head. "Danny."

Meanwhile, Danny is fast asleep.

The police show up an hour later with two very upset parents. Dad drags Danny out of bed, and it all goes down in the den. I sit on my toilet perch and listen to a lady scream at my brother for selling pods, each with as much nicotine as a pack of cigarettes, to her twelve-year-old. It seems like this mom has done her research.

It's strange, but I'm numb.

Danny refuses to tell them where he gets the vaping stuff. He's not old enough to buy it himself. He's going to be suspended for distributing to kids in our district, and he'll have to go to juvenile court or something like that.

"Is it the money, Dan?" Dad asks. "Is that what this is about?"

Danny doesn't say anything.

From my spot on the toilet, it's almost as if Danny isn't even there.

LETTER TO MY DECEASED GRANDPA, DANNY BOY

If dead people could accept mail, like if there were a glowing mail chute at the back of the cemetery that sucked up our letters with such force they made it to heaven, or wherever their souls are, I'd write a letter to my deceased grandpa. I would decorate the back with tiny photographs of cars from Danny's car magazines, because Mom always talks about how Grandpa loved cars. On the front, I would write this:

Dear Grandpa Dan,

Mom said you had a sense of humor, so you'll appreciate the fact that for eleven years I never drank more than a couple sips of anything at once, because I had heard you died from drinking too much, and I didn't want that to happen to me. Then in sixth-grade health class, I realized you died from drinking too much alcohol, which infected your liver. Weirdly, I still drink in small sips. It's a hard habit to break.

As you know, your timing is not good. Apparently, you were born on Pearl Harbor Day, two weeks before your own dad left for war (and never came back). And then you died two weeks before Danny was born. All of this made Mom nervous about bad things happening around babies' births. But then nothing happened when I was born, so that was a relief.

Anyway, Mom named Danny after you. She listened to your song, "Danny Boy," every day before and after he was born. I heard her tell Granny that she's scared she bathed Danny in sadness hormones, and that turned him into a sad child. Were you sad? I know everyone thought you were funny, but were you sad beneath it all? Is that why you drank too much?

I think if you were here with us, you and Danny would be great friends. He loves cars, too, and he's even funny sometimes. Maybe if you were here, you could talk to Mom and tell her not to be so worried all the time. Granny says if you were Danny's parent, you would smack him upside the ear. I don't know if smacking would work, but I'd love to see that.

Anyway, I hope heaven bathes you in happiness. And I hope you're waiting for Granny. She's afraid you might have a girlfriend up there.

> Love,
> Your Granddaughter Molly

WHEN YOU ACTUALLY MISS HAVING THE NICKNAME SNOT DROP BECAUSE THE ALTERNATIVE IS MORE HUMILIATING

We're usually running late, but this morning we're nice and early—early enough to eat avocado toast and drink one of Dad's famous decaf lattes. Mom drops me in front of a crowd of kids and tells me she loves me (like she has every morning since that lockdown). Nick is standing next to the lilac tree, and it seems weird to be smelling something beautiful while looking at Nick.

"Nice podcast, Swiss Alps," he says.

The seventh-grade Nick groupie next to him laughs and yells out, "Swiss Alps."

I have no clue what they're talking about.

I keep walking, relatively unfazed, because after nine years of dealing with Nick, I've pretty much learned to block him out. Swiss Alps is random and much less offensive than the nickname I got stuck with the entire winter of fourth grade, after Nick saw my nose was running on the way in from sledding at recess.

Snot Drop.

By the time I get to lunch, I've heard "Swiss Alps" a bunch of times combined with "*mumble, mumble,* stupid podcast." I think *Dress Coded: A Podcast* is starting to have an effect.

I sit at the end of our table, next to Navya and across

from Bea. Bea is eating a cold Big Mac and an ice cream cup, and Navya is stealing Doritos from Tom, because she's too lazy to wait in the long lunch line.

"Ashley is sitting with Rachel," Bea says.

"She swore to me she's not mad at us," Navya says. "She claims she's working on a social studies project with Rachel."

"Are we still going to her party?" Bea asks.

"Uh. Yes," Navya says.

"Nick is now calling me Swiss Alps," I say, digging around my backpack for my warm applesauce tube and my yogurt-covered energy bar.

Navya stops crunching and looks over at Bea. "That is so mean."

"Why is it mean?" I ask, watching Navya and Bea stare at each other. "I'm going to find out eventually. Just tell me."

"Okay, Molly," Navya says. "So we were talking about the physics of those cable cars that go up to the tops of mountains in science yesterday, and Mr. K. mentioned this mountain in Switzerland called Mount Titlis, and Nick and his annoying friends thought it was hilarious."

"Why?" Tom asks.

"It's not even worth explaining, Tom," Bea says.

"Oh. I thought it had something to do with the podcast," I say.

I'll never understand why when someone points out the one thing that makes you feel bad about yourself, your heart immediately hurts.

How does the heart know? I didn't tell it. Just like I'm never telling anyone how bad this makes me feel.

"Don't let it bother you. Nick is just being Nick," Navya says.

"Obviously," I say. "He's irrelevant."

My heart tells my throat. My throat tells my eyes. My eyes tell the tear ducts. And the notoriously cruel tear ducts betray me.

"Molly, are you crying? Oh my gosh, Moll, please. I'm so sorry I said anything." Bea moves closer and puts her arm around me. And now we've created a scene in the cafeteria, where scenes become major motion pictures.

"Stop, Bea," I say under my breath. "I'm just in a bad mood, and I'm literally crying about everything these days. I think I have a hormone imbalance."

"Oh my gosh, me too," Navya says.

"My mom told me there are too many hormones in our dairy products," Bea says.

"Maybe it's time to quit cheese." I dab my nose with a crumpled tissue from the bottom of my backpack.

One thing I learned from the winter of fourth grade when everybody called me Snot Drop was *always carry tissues*.

MY HEART TALKS TO MEGAN BIRCH BEHIND MY BACK

I am dreading science. What if the Mount Titlis thing is the topic of every science teacher's lesson? I sit next to Megan, take out my binder, and start organizing papers from two months ago.

"What's wrong?" Megan's face is two inches from mine.

"Nothing. Why?"

"Molly, give me a break. Obviously, you're upset about something."

I don't know how she knows, but it's as if she has a sixth sense.

"It's stupid. I'm having issues at home, and Ashley is ditching us because of the podcast, and Nick has been making fun of my bra size, and I have no idea why I'm letting it bother me."

"Oh," she says in kind of a weird way. I can't tell if she's judging me or sympathizing.

Mr. Lu comes in carrying a box full of pulleys and gears. He drops the box, which makes a loud crashing sound and scares half the class. It doesn't look like he's going to use Mount Titlis as an example, so I relax a little and try to figure out what he's attempting to do. Megan keeps licking her lips and looking over at me. She's writing in the back of her notebook.

Luckily, I'm not one of the seven people Mr. Lu calls up to demonstrate how a pulley works. I'm not in the mood to stand in front of the class, and I'm starving, because I forgot to eat lunch.

Megan rips out the last page of her notebook and slides it over to me. It's a list of over seventy words. Seventy horrible, hurtful, cruel words Nick has used to make fun of Megan's cerebral palsy.

I won't repeat them.

I won't give Nick that power.

Mr. Lu doesn't miss a beat. He's always on the lookout for phones and other contraband. "Molly and Megan, you want to share that note with the class?"

"Not really," I say.

He walks back anyway and grabs the piece of paper. I swear teachers all assume we're talking about them. He studies the note. "What is this?" He looks confused.

Megan smiles defiantly. "Those are all the words kids have used to describe me."

This girl is a human rocket ship, soaring through debris on her way to the stars.

Mr. Lu nods, slowly folds the paper, and sets it down on Megan's desk. "Sorry, kiddo."

It's obvious he has no idea what to say or do. He clears his throat and picks up the pulley. Megan and I use this rare opportunity to write notes back and forth. We're pretty sure Mr. Lu won't bother us again.

After class, Megan and I walk to our lockers together.

"Do you want to come over sometime?" she asks.

"Yes. Yes, I do."

She smiles, and I smile back.

I bet Nick has never known what it feels like to make a real friend.

WHEN YOU'RE HAVING AN H-E-DOUBLE-HOCKEY-STICKS DAY, YOU MIGHT AS WELL TAKE A PUCK TO THE FACE

Jessica, the senior, gets on the bus at the high school stop and says hi to Mary Kate before she leans down and whispers in my ear, "My friend Jasmine wants to do the podcast. I'll text you."

I check @DressCodedAPodcast on Instagram—140 more followers.

"I got dress coded today," Mary Kate says.

"What? Why?" She's wearing a T-shirt and jeans.

"Belly." She stands up, and a strip of flesh a millimeter wide peeks out between her shirt and pants.

"You must be kidding me. Who was it?"

"Fingertip."

"You okay?"

"Yeah. My friend Lucy got pulled over for having holes in her pants. Fingertip just kind of clumped me in with her because I was standing there. It was annoying."

I shake my head. "Hey, can I take a picture of your tiny strip of belly?"

"Go ahead."

She stands up again, and it takes me a while to get a good angle. I post a photo of Mary Kate's barely noticeable belly with the caption **#DressCoded for this much skin showing**.

Everybody's on the bus, scrolling through Instagram.

I get hundreds of likes in two minutes.

"Hey, Toad, you got any candy?" Danny asks from two seats behind us.

"Her name is Mary Kate," I shout back.

"And your name is Frog."

"Ribbit," I say, sticking out my tongue.

The bus stops, and I run toward the house. I rush upstairs and fling open my bedroom door.

I'm not prepared for what I find.

At first, I see the white dresses lying on my bed. Mom must have been in here looking at them. A second later, I hear something coming from my closet.

"Mom?"

She's sitting against the wall with her knees up to her chest, her eyes so swollen and red I can barely see them. Her hair is matted around her face, and she's rocking back and forth.

She holds the blue Play-Doh container in her hand.

"Mom?" I say again.

She closes her mouth tight and stares up at me.

"How could you?" she asks, with a squeaky voice.

"I just . . . I'm sorry. I don't know why . . ."

"All this time, I was focused on Danny. And you. My baby. You were doing it too." She starts to sob.

"Wait," I say. "What? You think *I'm* doing it? Mom, it's not mine." The words fly out before I can catch them, before I realize how much I sound like every bad movie when the teenager gets caught.

"How could you, Molly? After everything we've been through."

I stare down at the purple slime stain on my fuzzy rug and feel my mind go absolutely blank.

She crawls out on her hands and knees, covered in snot and tears, and pulls herself up. She stumbles and gathers up the pods, the cash, the containers, all the rubble left by my brother's disgusting habit.

"Mom?" It's all I can say.

"Don't you talk to me."

She drags my old slime kit out of my room and barrels down the hallway. I hear a loud crash and see her face full of rage as the kit tumbles down the stairs.

I lie down on my bed and pull the covers over me.

She's too mad to listen to me. She knows I can't stand Danny. Why should she believe I would let him store his stuff in my room? And even if she does believe me, what will happen to Danny? This could be the thing that finally gets him sent to one of those "programs" for bad kids I've seen bookmarked on Mom's laptop. Or worse, this could be the reason my parents move our family, like they've whispered about so many times.

Danny walks past my room and quietly closes his door.

CONSEQUENCES

I'm grounded until summer.

I can't go on the camping trip.

My phone is gone.

I can't go to Ashley's birthday party Saturday.

"What about my podcast?" I asked.

"Fine," they said.

Mom is giving me the silent treatment. Dad came into my room, sat on my bed, and licked his fingers as he riffled through printouts of articles talking about the health risks of vaping.

"Take a look at these, and then we'll talk," he said.

I don't know why I'm having so much trouble sticking up for myself. My words are stuck there, in my throat, like a congealed truth ball.

Right now, all I have is *Dress Coded: A Podcast*, a ton of homework I can't focus on, and a brother who is letting me lose everything for something I didn't do.

I torture him by playing the same song over and over again on my clarinet.

Oh, Danny Boy, the pipes, the pipes are calling . . .

IN THE MORNING

Danny comes in at around six and taps me on the head repeatedly until I wake up.

"What, Danny?"

"I'm sorry this happened. Thanks for taking one for the team," he whispers.

He sits on the edge of my bed.

"I'm not taking one for the team. I'm trying to keep our family from moving out of the country. Mom and Dad talk about it, you know."

"I've been a bad brother, and I get it. I just want you to know I'm sorry. I really didn't want to drag you into this."

I actually think he means it. "Okay. Can you stop now? It's not worth it. Just stop."

"I'm going to. I'm done with vaping and selling. I don't care about it anymore anyway."

"Good."

"You're a pretty cool kid, Moll."

I can't believe he just said that.

"Thanks, Danny." I turn over and pull up the covers. I feel a frog (and a toad) hopping around on my heart.

o o o

Mom still says "I love you" when she drops me off. I say it back, and my insides twist around like a snake stuck in a lunch box.

DRESS CODED: A PODCAST

ME: Hello, Fisher Middle School and beyond. My name is Molly Frost, and this is *Dress Coded: A Podcast*, episode five. Today, I'm talking to Lucy P., seventh grader, basketball player, and chess club treasurer. Lucy, do you want to tell me a little about yourself?

LUCY: Um, other than basketball and chess club, I'm a student rep, so I'll be helping out with Moving Up Day, and I've always been obsessed with bats.

ME: Baseball or furry flying creatures?

LUCY: *[Laughs.]* Furry flying creatures. Did you know the average bat consumes a thousand mosquitoes in a single hour? My neighbor built a bat house after I told him that.

ME: That's pretty fascinating. So my neighbor Mary Kate, who is also here with us today, told me you got pulled over for wearing ripped jeans.

LUCY: Yes. And they weren't even that ripped. They're the exact same jeans another friend of mine wore yesterday, and nobody said anything to her.

ME: Why do you think that is?

LUCY: Because teachers love her.

ME: That's not fair.

LUCY: I know. Fingertip told me I looked like my pants went through a paper shredder.

ME: Wow. Very original. So how did that make you feel?

LUCY: Furious. Then she stared at Mary Kate, trying to find something wrong with what she was wearing. She finally found, like, a speck of skin showing and yelled at her.

MARY KATE: You can see the evidence on Instagram and decide for yourself if I was dressed inappropriately.

ME: Listeners, you can post your own pictures on Instagram using hashtag Dress Coded. So, Lucy, if you could say one thing to the teachers at Fisher Middle, what would it be?

LUCY: Hmm. Leave us alone.

ME: That about sums it up.

o o o

"That was kind of short," Mary Kate says.

"It was perfect," I say, checking to make sure everything recorded. "Hey, can you hang out for a while? You're my only contact with human beings outside of school."

"I can't believe you're letting Danny do this to you."

"I don't want to move away."

"You can stay here and live with me."

"Thanks, but I like TV too much."

Mary Kate and I check the Instagram page.

People from other towns are posting their own pictures.

#DressCoded for too much thigh.

#DressCoded for having shoulders.

#DressCoded for being a mammal.

This is so much bigger than Fisher Middle School.

I SEE WHY AMERICANS SPEND BILLIONS
ON INSOMNIA MEDICATIONS

Three days in a row, I run extra hard at lacrosse practice to make myself tired so I can go home, do my homework, eat, and sleep. But all three nights I end up falling asleep in my sweaty clothes before dinner and then waking up and staying wide-awake until two in the morning.

The first night, I stare out the window at the blinking streetlight and wonder how I will possibly survive the summer.

The second night, I clean out my drawers and make a photo wall with all the pictures I've taken of my friends this year. I make Thibodeaux model in the moonlight until I can get a good picture of him, even though his expression says *Why am I standing here wearing sunglasses under a makeup lamp at midnight? No dog treat is worth this.*

The third night, I try to work on my history project but realize it's impossible to do schoolwork in the middle of the night, no matter how wide-awake I am.

I stick my binder in the nightstand drawer and attempt to will myself to sleep until Danny opens the door and creeps in.

"What are you doing?" I say, acting groggy, like he woke me up.

"Nothing. Go back to sleep."

He gets on his hands and knees, crawls into my closet, and starts blurting out curse words.

He's looking for pods.

By the light of the flickering streetlamp, I witness my brother crawl out of the closet with a vape pod, puncture it with a nail file, and start sucking on it. This is what he's become, now that Mom has all his devices.

Our health teacher taught us about the terrible things people do when their body craves whatever they are addicted to. Sucking on a pod wasn't one of them.

"Get out right now, or I'm screaming for Mom and Dad."

He crawls away.

DRESS SHOPPING WITH A STOMACHACHE

It's Saturday, the day of Ashley's party. I'm picturing my friends' floors littered with bikini tops and bottoms and nail polish bottles, while I sit on my own floor drawing hearts on my leg with a green pen.

Danny is out of control. All his pods and money are gone, and he needs nicotine to be normal. He's downstairs screaming at Dad, and I'm stuck in my room until my lacrosse game, where I'll get to hear about the party until I explode with rage.

Mom comes in and stands over me. Her face is thin and pinched. Granny used to say, "Don't cross your eyes. They'll stay that way." But she should have been telling her daughter, "Don't make a pinched face when you think your children are vaping, or it will stay that way."

"I returned the dresses for you."

"You did? But you hate going to the post office."

"These days, going to the post office is better than being home."

Nice, Mom.

"What was wrong with them, anyway?"

"The dresses?"

"Yes, the dresses, Molly."

She hates me.

"They were all too big."

"Let's go out in a few minutes and get a dress so I don't have to worry about this," she says.

"I have a game."

"Not until four. Get ready."

"Can I still get Ashley a present even if I'm not going to the party?"

"I guess so, Molly."

When Mom is mad at me, my stomach hurts. It's like heartache, but a little lower.

∘ ∘ ∘

Mom passes Marshalls and Kohl's, and keeps going, toward downtown Hartford. She pulls into the parking lot of the fancy store where I got my flower girl dress for Aunt Maggie's wedding. "We don't need to go here," I say.

"I just want to get it over with." She slams the car door shut. "I'm done with this district loading all these added expenses on us."

A nice old lady shows us the in-between sizes. "This is why they call you tweens," she says, rubbing my arm.

Mom and I ignore the comment. What's the point of telling her I'm already fourteen? Mom sits on a tufted bench outside the dressing room as I try on dress after dress. Some are garbage bags, some are blah, some look more like christening gowns than graduation dresses.

"You shouldn't write on yourself," the lady says, pointing to the green hearts dotting the landscape of my skin.

"Yeah, that's what my granny says."

"Here, try this one."

I know the second I slip it over my head. It's strapless but flattering, just the right length, and edged with a tiny bit of lace. It's the most beautiful piece of clothing I've ever worn.

"It's gorgeous, honey," Mom says, and I can tell she's forgotten she's furious for a second.

"Thanks, Mom."

"How much is it?"

"Two twenty, on sale from four twenty-five," the lady says, with her cold fingers against my back as she squints at the price tag. "Final sale, so no returns."

Mom's face drops.

"It's okay, Mom. We'll find another good one."

I know we won't, because my nine-year-old body deserves a nine-year-old's dress.

Mom bursts into tears, and the old lady hands her a tissue.

"No worries," the lady says. "We can find one to work with your budget."

"We'll take it." Mom wipes her nose and searches her bag for her wallet.

"No, Mom." I feel awful.

"I'll give it to you for two hundred even, sweetie." The lady puts the dress on a satin hanger and pulls a garment bag over it.

"I'd like you to start seeing the therapist again," Mom says when we're back in the car.

"Okay."

My stomach hurts so bad I ask Mom to text my coach. I can't go to the game. I can't ask for more money to buy Ashley a gift. I can't even look my mother in the eye. I go up to my bed and sleep through all the splashing and dancing and pizza eating that must be happening at the party.

I wake up at two a.m.

Again.

WHEN ENCOUNTERING A HEADLESS BIRD
IS THE HIGHLIGHT OF YOUR DAY

Mom asks me to walk Tibby, which I usually hate doing on Sunday morning, because all the neighbors are out gardening and they want me to stop and talk. But today I grab the leash and go. I'm just glad to be out in civilization.

I walk through the woods to the back of the school and cut through Will's yard. Tibby stops to sniff a headless bird lying next to the picnic table. I don't even want to think about what kind of creature eats a bird's head and keeps going.

"What are you doing?" Will shouts from his bedroom window.

"I'm walking Thibodeaux. Come down."

He appears five minutes later, wearing pajamas four inches too short.

"Nice soccer ball pj's," I say.

"Thanks." He takes a bite of a banana. "Oh, man. What is that?"

"A headless bird. Tibby wants at it."

"That is terrifying."

"I know."

We stare at the bird, trying to figure out what could have happened.

Satanic ritual. Hawk. Rat. Coyote. Bear. Creepy person. Rare degenerative disease that only affects bird heads. Ran into a tree, lost head, and body kept flying for a while.

That gets boring, and I ask Will about Ashley's party. He didn't go, but Clay and Rahul watched the whole thing unfold on social media.

"Let's see, apparently they danced. They got into a Jell-O fight. Bea was crying because somebody knocked her phone into the pool. It sounded like they had some pretty good food. And a bunch of people were vaping in the lawn-mower shed."

"That's it?"

"I don't know. What else could have happened?"

He has a good point.

"Why are you grounded? I don't ever remember you being grounded."

"You don't want to know."

"It's that bad?"

"Worse. I didn't do anything."

He stares at me and pushes Tibby away, because Tibby has an annoying habit of licking people's feet. "You're covering for Danny."

"Yup. I don't want to move."

"Your parents are never going to move."

"You don't know that."

"Molly, your dad isn't going to quit his job and move to another country because Danny vapes. Believe me, my dad was researching to see if any towns in America have banned all video games. Parents just get stressed-out."

I bend down and study the bird. It's a female cardinal. Dad used to teach us about birds before we had to get rid of the bird feeders, now called "bear feeders" in our town.

"Hey, do you think you're covering for him because maybe, just maybe, he'll be nice to you?"

"He has been a lot nicer to me. I mean, he's not hitting me or calling me ugly."

"Dude, he's never going to be the kind of brother you want. There's no point ruining your life over something that is never happening."

"You sound like an adult."

"A five-year-old could tell you something this obvious. He refers to you as *a frog*."

"Only when I'm with Mary Kate."

"Oh. Okay, Molly."

I yank Tibby away from the headless bird. "We should give her a proper burial."

We tie Tibby to the deck railing and dig a hole under a tree in the woods between Will's house and mine. Will carefully pushes her onto the shovel with a garden hoe and sets her in our hole. We cover her with dirt and leaves and more dirt, and set a bunch of rocks on top so Tibby doesn't get loose and dig her up later to finish her off.

"Rest in peace, headless bird," Will says.

"I wonder what the best day of her life was. Like was it a sunny day when the flowers were blooming and she flew all over town looking for plump worms? Or maybe she had babies and it was the day they hatched."

"They may not have all hatched in one day."

"Whatever, Will."

"Well, we know the worst day of her life, that's for sure."

Tibby whines to go home, so I take him. I walk in to find Dad yelling at Danny while Mom sits on the floor in the mudroom.

"Come on, Thibodeaux," I say. "Let's have breakfast."

THE BEST DAY OF MY LIFE (SO FAR)

When I was eight and Danny was eleven, Granny treated all of us and Aunt Maggie and our little cousins to a trip to Atlantis in the Bahamas. Mom surprised us by showing us commercials of people flying down water slides and playing on the beach. "Do you want to go there?" she asked. "Yes!" we yelled. "Now?" she asked.

We nearly fainted.

Dad appeared from the other room with our suitcases and passports.

Our cousins were toddlers, so they spent their time playing in the sand and splashing around the kiddie pool while Danny and I explored the whole resort by ourselves. We watched the stingrays and the giant sea turtles. We floated down the lazy river holding hands, because Dad said we had to stay together. We did karaoke at the kids' club and took a cooking class, and stayed up until midnight watching movies with the other kids.

The day before we left, it rained so hard we thought a hurricane was coming to swallow us up. So we went down to the basement of the hotel and discovered the real Atlantis—secret tunnels under the sea, where we played among the fish and artifacts until Granny eventually found us and dragged us to the buffet.

"Never tell anyone we found Atlantis," Danny said.

"I promise."

We linked pinky fingers, and for the first time, I felt like my brother loved me.

That whole day, he didn't tell me how annoying I was or smack me or kick me, or pin me down and spit in my face. He didn't threaten me or tell me I was ugly.

That day we found the real Atlantis was the best day of my life. If a giant creature swoops in and eats my head, that day will stay with my (freaked-out) soul for all eternity.

MY BIGGEST FEAR

That the best days of my life have already passed.

WHAT COULD BE WORSE THAN
THE STOMACH BUG?

"Danny? Let me in," Mom yells from the hallway.

My clock says 12:44 a.m.

"Danny. I need to get in there."

The door hinges squeak open. "Oh, hon. Let me help you."

Every five minutes, Danny makes a horrible sound as his body tries to throw up, but there's nothing left in his stomach. I stick my head in and see Mom rubbing Danny's back as he hangs off the bed over his Teenage Mutant Ninja Turtles trash can.

Dad drives out to the pharmacy for Pepto, ginger ale, and saltines.

I literally stick my fingers in my ears and try to sleep this way, and then I start wondering if anyone in the history of the planet has ever been able to fall asleep with their fingers in their ears.

"He's asleep, poor buddy," Mom says to Dad. I suddenly realize Mom probably likes Danny being sick. She can rub his back and take care of him and feel needed.

Dad lumbers downstairs (he's always so loud on the stairs, even in socks), and I hear Mom shut Danny's squeaky door most of the way.

"Mom, can you come in?" I ask.

"Oh no. Do you have the bug too, hon?"

"It's not a bug, Mom."

"What?"

"It's not a bug. He's nic-sick. He needs nicotine." I say it dryly, like I'm telling her he needs toilet paper or a new marble notebook.

She sways a little and then comes over to my bed, pulls up the comforter, and crawls in. She faces me and awkwardly wraps her arms around me, and presses her forehead against mine like she did when I was little.

"What did I do wrong, Molly?" Her breath smells like saltines.

I pull away a little. "Mom, I have to tell you something."

She listens calmly as I tell her about the slime kit and the Play-Doh containers and how Danny has been nicer to me and how I didn't want that to stop. I think of our Candy Land tournament and the times he sat on my bed asking me random questions, and I tell it all to Mom because all the secrets and lies are sticking to my soul like bits of glass.

I need my mom back.

She apologizes too many times, and I make her stop, because it's getting annoying.

"Why didn't you just tell me?" she asks.

"I'm so scared you're going to make us move. I've heard you talking about it."

"Oh, honey. I talk like that when I'm panicking. Sometimes I just need to feel like we have an out."

"Danny needs help, Mom. But taking me away from my friends and my life wouldn't be fair."

"I know, Moll."

I promise her no more covering up. No more secrets. She promises me she'll figure this out and we won't move. She tells me she's proud of me for my podcast and for being a great kid. I fall asleep with her arms around me, which is much easier than falling asleep with my fingers in my ears.

In the morning, she brushes the hair away from my face and kisses me on the forehead. "I guess I'll cancel the therapist today."

"No. Let's wait until summer vacation. But I still want to go."

CONSEQUENCES

I'm ungrounded.

I can go on the camping trip.

My phone is back.

I can invite Ashley to a double sleepover because I missed her party (and hopefully make things better between us).

Danny flings open my door and calls me a gross, ugly narc. Tibby sits up on my bed and wags his tail, obliviously happy that Danny's giving us attention.

I did what he asked because I wanted him to like me. But he never actually liked me. He let me get in trouble. He didn't say a word. He used me.

I'll never have my fountain brother.

It's time for me to stop wishing.

Memorial Day is big in our town. I don't know if it always was, but it has been ever since four people passed away in the First Gulf War. That's a lot of people from one town.

Danny is still in bed. Mom and Dad are talking out in the car so we don't hear them. Tibby is licking his paw, something he does when he's stressed-out. And I'm standing by the window in my scratchy band uniform, waiting for Bea to pick me up. (My reed is split and I don't have another one, so I'll be fake-playing.)

Bea's phone is dead, so I'm forced to text her dad's phone.

> **ME: Hi, it's Molly. What time should I be ready?**

> **BEA'S DAD:** 10 is dandy.

> **ME: Thanks.**

> **BEA'S DAD:** Cool, dude!

Every parade I've been in since Daisies has involved an uncomfortable outfit: Girl Scout uniform, junior band uniform, and now the sweltering Fisher Middle School band uniform, made of lizard skin and fire embers.

It's hot. And it's only going to get hotter.

Bea's dad is tall, dark, and handsome (for a dad). He ruins it with his weirdness.

"And the band's all here," he says, waving to Mom and Dad, who are getting out of their car. "Were they out getting bagels? I see your pops over at the bagel place sometimes."

"Yeah," I say, because it's a lot easier than saying *No, they locked themselves in the car and were plotting what to do with a seventeen-year-old nicotine addict.*

In the back seat, Bea is cleaning out her flute. She pulls out black grossness and rubs it on me. I'm too tired to care.

Bea's dad takes the shortcut to avoid parade traffic, which probably ends up taking longer. We jump out on the corner and make our way over to the cluster of miserable middle schoolers who are all definitely thinking the same thing: *Why did I let my parents talk me into playing a musical instrument because it supposedly looks good on a college application?*

Olivia and Pearl wave us over, and we huddle under a scrawny tree to avoid the sun. Mrs. Winslow claps her hands and manages to get us into marching formation. I'm next to Olivia, who actually plays her clarinet.

We shuffle to Main Street and file in behind the volunteer firefighters. I recognize a couple of them from the time they rescued four chipmunk babies from the storm drain after Mary Kate called 911.

We begin our song, which we will play four times between here and Fisher Middle School. *My country 'tis of thee, sweet land of liberty, of thee I sing.* (I hum the words as I pretend to play.) The high school band gets to play "America the Beautiful." I'm thinking this will be my last year of clarinet.

People sit in lawn chairs on both sides of Main Street. Out of the corner of my eye, I spot a lady dumping bottled water on her head. The lady next to her is trying to fan her face with a little American flag. I focus on putting one foot in front of the other and remind myself this is a twelve-minute walk. Soldiers have to do this for hundreds, maybe thousands, of miles.

We end on the lawn next to the FMS garden. The interim superintendent is sitting on the stage, reading something. I'm pretty sure it's not our petition. I wish I had the nerve to go up and ask him why he hasn't responded. Dr. Couchman is there, with his red face and his goofy grin. He's trying to talk to the state legislator, but the state legislator is ignoring him.

The head of the town council goes up to the podium, and Bea and I scramble to sit under the pop-up tent where two Korean War veterans are selling paper poppies for one dollar each.

"I would buy one," I tell them, "but my band pants don't have pockets, so I don't have a dollar." They give me one anyway, and I wrap the wire around my finger.

The state legislator talks for an eternity. The chief of police talks for an eternity. Then a lady gets up to the podium. She's tiny, and somebody runs up to adjust the mic. The lady stands there holding a lilac.

The whole field goes silent.

She holds the lilac to her nose and says, "Back when this school was being built, the planners came to me and said, 'Lydia, how would you like Violeta to be remembered?' Vi, you see, was my baby girl. She was a scout, an athlete, a scholar, a soldier, and a hero. She died trying to pull a baby boy out of a blown-up building.

"How do I want Violeta remembered? With deeds. 'Deeds, not words, Mom,' Vi always said. The mothers of Aaron and Jamie and Justin and I would sit out here in this field, and we would remember our children. Sometimes we brought each other flowers, because flowers really do comfort the mothers of the dead.

"'Flowers,' we all said. 'That's what this new school needs.' And we got on our hands and knees and dug and planted and tilled and watered until our garden grew." She holds the lilac up to her forehead and closes her eyes. "I like to think Violeta and the boys are with us here. Maybe they are the ones who draw the bees and butterflies to the blooms. Maybe they are the real keepers of this garden, and we're just their silly moms who come to talk and weed and dump a little fertilizer now and then."

She waves the other moms up and passes out lilacs to the mothers of Aaron and Jamie and Justin. They embrace, and everyone is sobbing, I mean everyone, even the legislator and the chief of police.

Ms. Milholland, the old FMS principal, rises to her feet and claps. People stand and clap all around her.

"Deeds, everyone," Violeta's mom says. "That's how we remember our babies. Go forth, make your voices heard, and do good."

Chills run through me.

I think I finally get the point of Memorial Day.

Mom's on the front porch when I get home. She hands me a tall glass of iced tea. I rip my uniform jacket off and sit on the step in my tank top.

"Molly, I just want you to know how sorry I am for everything."

"I know, Mom. You don't have to apologize anymore. I'm sorry for hiding Danny's stuff."

"I spoke to Ashley's mom. She was very understanding. She would love to host the double sleepover at her house this weekend."

"Why did you tell her about Danny?"

"I'm sick of hiding it."

Mom trusts people too much. She doesn't realize how judgmental Ashley's mom is and that she's "happy to host" because she doesn't want her kid over here associating with that maniac Danny Frost.

"I just want to be normal again," I say.

She smiles. "How about we shoot for almost normal?"

We stack the counter with whatever is in the fridge: half-thawed blueberries, chocolate chip cookie dough, carrots, eggs, and frozen alphabet fries. We text Will's mom, and Dad and Will's dad bring the picnic tables together in our yard. We spread out our checkered tablecloths and feast on deviled eggs, carrots dipped in ranch dressing, warm pound cake with cold blueberries, alphabet fries, and half a lasagna (from Will's fridge). Dad builds a fire in the firepit, and the parents sit around and talk while Will and I lie in our spots in the stuffy tree house and try to imagine what life will be like in ninth grade.

"The same as it is now," Will predicts.

"Almost the same but better."

"I like Pearl."

"This again?"

"I'm sorry. I think I'm in love with her."

I can tell it's serious by the way his lip quivers a little. "Wow. Okay. I'll see what I can do."

"Thanks."

Mom shouts up, "Molly, can you guys bring a plate up to Dan? He hasn't eaten all day."

Will and I fill a plate with blueberries and cake and two chocolate chip cookies. (Danny despises most non-dessert foods.) We pass Will's dad, who is smoking a cigarette behind the toolshed, and run up to Danny's room.

He's not there.

HOW WE TRY TO FIND MY BROTHER

- Search the whole house.
- Call his friends.
- Search the neighborhood.
- Call his acquaintances.
- Split up and drive around.
- Fly Will's drone over the entire county. (This plan fails after Will tells us the drone needs to charge and it won't be ready until tomorrow.)

WHEN PRINCE WILLISTER AND PRINCESS MOLLIFLOWER END UP EATING COOKIES IN THE DARK

I ride with Dad. He doesn't say much as his eyes scan the streets. There aren't a lot of people out on Memorial Day night—just a few houses with a lot of cars in front of them and then quiet. TVs are on; people are walking around their kitchens, getting ready for school and work tomorrow. A shirtless man waters his lawn, and the sun sets in tie-dye over our town.

"Can we get ice cream?" I ask. I'm not that worried about Danny. I think he's out trying to get pods.

"Not right now, Molls. Let's go after we find Danny."

We drive around for hours, circling back three, then four, then five times.

"We could have made it to Granny's by now," I say.

"Yep." Dad chews on his Dunkin' Donuts straw.

We don't find Danny.

We stand in the driveway with Will's family and debate whether it's time to call the police. It starts to rain. It's a hot rain, not strong enough to scare away the mosquitoes. Mom wants to call the police. Dad wants to wait. Will's parents help them weigh the pros and cons, and it's kind of nice to be with them again, like we were all the time before things got difficult.

Danny comes walking up the driveway like nothing's wrong.

"What's up?" he asks.

"Oh, come on, Dan," Dad says.

"Why don't you get your stuff and spend the night with us, Molly?" Will's mom says.

I used to ask Mom, "Will I ever be able to have a sleepover on a school night?"

"Maybe someday," she always said.

Sleeping alone in a guest room with grimy teeth, because I forgot my toothbrush, was not what I had in mind.

When we first got phones, Will's mom and my mom decided they would take our phones every night at ten for the rest of our lives, and they've stuck with that decision. But tonight, with a missing person and a last-minute sleepover, Will's mom forgets to take my phone. So we're hunched over my phone on the bathroom floor on the 217-person group chat trying to sort out who will be sharing tents. Megan Birch asked if she could sleep in our tent (since her best friend is a boy who goes to another school). I said yes without checking with Bea, Ashley, and Navya, and they got mad, because it will be too hot and crowded (and because none of them have ever talked to Megan). So now I'm planning to do a two-woman tent with Megan, which will probably be better, because Navya has a serious snoring problem. She snores like an old man who swallowed a piglet who swallowed a horn.

Are Molly and Will having a sleepover? Will's buddy Clay texts.

We're neighbors. Duh.

Snap Map gives every secret away. I disable and turn off my phone.

We don't need this tonight. It would be fuel for Nick, who will tell everyone Swiss Alps is having a sleepover with Deformity, which is the uncreative name Nick came up with because Will has a pinkish-purple Florida-shaped birthmark on his cheek. Back when our tree house was a keep, Will's birthmark was the mark of a prince chosen by the goddess tribunal. Prince Willister presided over a kingdom of gnomes and gargoyles. As ruler of the northern forests, the prince met at the keep with Princess Molliflower, ruler of the southern gardens, to discuss invading armies and rains damaging the sugarplum crops.

But at school, Prince Willister was known by the name Deformity.

Will stands up in his too-short soccer-ball pajamas.

"Good save," he says. "Clay loves to cause drama."

"Always has."

"Do you want me to go down and get some cookies and milk?"

"I'll come with you."

We tiptoe down the carpeted stairs and sit at the kitchen table, dunking cookies in milk by the light of the moon. We don't need to talk about it. I don't need to cry on his shoulder and tell him I'm scared for Danny and worried about my parents and sick of all the fighting and stress. He knows.

Sometimes eating cookies with a best friend in the middle of the night is better than talking.

On the way upstairs, Will whispers, "Don't forget about that Pearl thing."

He really is in love.

WHEN A WATCH BECOMES A WARNING AT THE PERFECT MOMENT TO SAVE YOU FROM A POTENTIAL FISTFIGHT WITH A TEACHER

We're under a tornado watch, and all Fingertip can think to do is dress code people who are so hot they can barely function. It is ninety-seven degrees in the shade, and the air is so sticky you could catch flies with it, but shoulders are going to take down the world. They're not the only ones—the belly girls, the too-much-thigh girls, the bra-strap girls—they're all getting it today.

Navya got called out of Spanish class. Now she's crying in the bathroom, because she missed test review and she's already practically failing Spanish. Navya is also petrified of tornadoes.

"I think I'm having a panic attack," she says, bending over to try to catch her breath.

Two seventh graders are vaping in the corner and staring at us as I wet a bunch of paper towels with cold water and press them against the back of her neck. "I'll find somebody who has good notes, and we can meet after school. It's okay. We'll handle it."

Our phones all make beeping sounds. I pull mine out of my backpack.

Tornado watch in effect until 5:00 p.m. today.

"It's a watch, not a warning," one of the seventh graders says.

"If you keep vaping, you'll wish you were killed by a tornado," I say. I can't help myself. The girl's eyes get wide, and she and her friend make a quick exit.

"Come on, honey bunny, let's go get some water." I hold Navya gently by the back of the arm and lead her to the good fountain, the one with more than a trickle. I fill her metal water bottle, and she takes a few sips.

"Girls, what's the holdup?" I don't even have to turn around to recognize Mr. Dern's voice. "Is it spring fever? It that why you're all violating dress code today? Come on— down to the office."

Navya turns and stares at him with her bright-pink face still streaked with mascara.

Beep beep beep. Dern's phone is reminding us of the tornado watch.

"Let's go. Office," he says, and then turns to me. "And you get back to class."

"She's already been to the office," I say. "She's going back to class."

"They didn't ask your parents to bring you a change of clothes?"

"I got a first warning."

"Well, put a sweatshirt on."

"It's a hundred degrees!" I shout. "What is wrong with you?" I've had it.

"What's your name?"

"My name is Molly Frost. I was in your advisory last year."
Beep. Beep. Beep.

Saved by the beep. Couchman gets on the loudspeaker and tells everyone the skies are looking ominous and they've changed the watch to a warning, so they're going to implement the tornado protocol. The halls flood with teachers asking one another "What's the tornado protocol again?" And Dern is swallowed up by a bunch of faculty complaining that Couchman didn't do a good job training them for this.

If the sky were a mascara color, it would be charcoal pewter. Navya grabs my backpack and yanks me back into the bathroom. She kneels down under the sink and covers her head with her hands. "It's like what happened at that Missouri school all over again," she says.

"It's not. We're surrounded by mountains. We'll be fine."

I convince her to go back to Spanish, and I go next door to science, where Mr. Lu is securing the lab equipment while everyone else sweats in uncomfortable pretzel-like positions under the tables. He makes us shut off our phones, because he can no longer tolerate the beeps and, even more annoying, the calls from scared parents.

And then it's over.

The skies clear, the light returns, and we get dismissed.

Mom is there to pick me up. I guess Danny being missing made it that much easier for her to imagine me being carried away by a tornado as I clung to the leg of a Fisher Middle School science table.

"A level-one tornado touched down a couple towns away," Mom says.

"Why don't they name tornadoes like they do hurricanes?"

"I don't know."

"Well, they should."

THINGS MOM AND I DO TO KILL AN HOUR BECAUSE DAD IS HOME WITH DANNY AND WE NEED A BREAK

- Share a lemon bar and a Venti iced tea at Starbucks to celebrate the fact we didn't get killed by Zoe, our first named tornado— we started the alphabet backward.
- Use our 20-percent-off Bed Bath & Beyond coupon to buy a new bath mat for Danny's bathroom.
- Get gas (and buy frozen dinners at the gas station).
- Sit in the car and scroll through Mom's Facebook.
- Decide we're going to take a road trip this summer (just the two of us).

HOW DO YOU SAY "HEARTBREAK" IN SPANISH? (ASKING FOR A FRIEND)

Pearl agrees to come over to help Navya with Spanish. It's still raining hard and I'm trying to focus on my English essay, but Navya is struggling and Pearl is trying to be patient.

"I'm not in the mood to do this right now," Navya says. "But thanks for trying to shove this into my thick head, Pearl."

"You know more than you think." Pearl gathers up her hair and puts it in a ponytail. She is really pretty. I can see why Will is obsessed.

Will. I almost forgot.

"Why can't school be over already?" Navya says. "Oh, and I can't believe I was dress coded today."

"Can I take a picture?" I ask.

She sticks her tongue out, and I post the picture of Navya in her tank top. **#DressCoded for wearing a tank top on a 97-degree day.**

"I saw this article online about a group of girls who posted signs all over their school with anti-dress-coding slogans. We should do that," Pearl says. "I bet Bea could make some amazing rebel art."

"Hmm. That's a great idea. We could make a bunch of signs and hang them after lacrosse practice," I say.

"Let's do it," Navya says, packing up her stuff. She exits through the hatch and runs home to get ready for indoor practice. (The last thing I feel like doing is going to lacrosse practice at five thirty on a rainy night.)

"Hey, Pearl, can I tell you something?"

"Yeah."

"So this is kind of awkward, and you don't have to say anything right now, but Will has a serious crush on you."

She sits back against the wall and blinks her eyes a bunch of times.

"Really? I seriously had no idea. I mean, he's nice to me in class, but he's always been a nice kid."

"He's pretty great." I wish Prince Willister could hear me talking him up. "So . . . thoughts?"

She smiles. I never realized her braces were blue.

"I kind of like somebody else, but I absolutely can't tell you right now."

"Why not? I promise I'll tell you if and when I ever like anyone."

She smiles again, and her cheeks turn pink.

"Not yet. But please, please tell Will he's super cute and a really nice guy."

I won't be mentioning this conversation to Will today or ever.

"Hint?"

"Nope."

"Okay, fine. Let's meet here tomorrow to make our signs."

"I'll be here."

Will needs to find someone else to fall in love with.

HOW I FELL IN LIKE WITH NAVYA

We always talk about falling in love with people, but it's much more common to fall in like with people.

I knew Navya before she showed up in my fifth-grade class. We took ice-skating lessons at the skating center together back when she was still at the Montessori school. Her face relaxed when our teacher introduced her as Navya from Montessori and she looked around the room and saw me. I grabbed her hand and dragged her to lunch and recess, and she sat with Olivia, Bea, and me every day. But that's not when I fell in like.

I fell in like with Navya from Montessori and ice skating when she stood up and walked to the front of the classroom carrying a lacrosse stick, a ball, and a love for a sport I had never even really heard of. Her face glowed as she told us about Native Americans playing with deerskin balls stuffed with hair. Back then, she said, the game was a way to keep the peace. She talked about the history of women's lacrosse. She said she learned the game from her mom, who played in college, and she plays all year because her day doesn't feel normal if she doesn't play lacrosse.

I was only in fifth grade, but Navya made me want to be that passionate about something someday. Navya was so happy and excited to talk about lacrosse, she made me fall in like with her.

I wanted her to be my best friend.

Navya is the best lacrosse player our coach has ever seen, and that includes the boys. She even managed to teach me, and I'm a klutz. "It's like ice skating," she always said when I was running around her backyard like a lost chicken. "It takes a little while to get the hang of it."

I didn't tell her I took ice-skating lessons for six years.

I never got the hang of it.

OUT OF SORTS IS ANOTHER TERM FOR "MY BROTHER HAS ALWAYS BEEN MEAN TO ME"

Mom, Dad, Will's dad, and Danny are at the kitchen table when I get back from lacrosse. I chug two glasses of lemonade and am instantly hit with lemonade-stomachache syndrome.

They all look at me.

"You want to come sit a minute?" Mom asks.

I look at Danny, who is staring at the uneaten slice of pizza on his plate.

"So Dan is going to go down to Granny's with Dad for a bit," Mom says.

"Why?" I ask.

Dad looks over at Will's dad. "We're going to go to a doctor who lives in Westchester, near Granny. She specializes in addiction."

Danny shakes his head. "This is ridiculous."

"She's an amazing doctor, Danny," Will's dad says. "Our friends had a great experience with her. Come on, man. You don't want to be messing around with pods thirty years from now, like I am with cigarettes. I could buy a Ferrari with the money I've wasted."

"Okay, Roger. You can go home now," Danny says.

"Danny, you are not going to be rude to Roger. He's here trying to help," Mom says.

"I don't need help. I need less psychotic parents. And a less ugly sister."

The lemonade stomachache turns into a family-stress stomachache.

"I have a lot of homework," I say. I grab my backpack, run upstairs, and collapse on the bed.

Mom comes in a little while later. "I just want you to know he's doing this because he's out of sorts."

"He's been out of sorts since I was born, Mom."

Her face drops, and she walks out to pack Danny's suitcase, because Danny is out of sorts and can't do anything for himself.

THINGS DAD WAS PLANNING TO DO DURING HIS TWO WEEKS OFF

- Golf.
- Clean out the garage.
- Clean up the yard.
- Make some playlists for me.
- Take me kayaking, like we do every year right before school is out.
- Maybe sleep in a few days.
- Bake popovers (my favorite).

THINGS DAD IS ACTUALLY DOING
DURING HIS TWO WEEKS OFF

- Getting yelled at by his mother-in-law for splashing water all over the floor when he takes a shower in her tiny bathroom.
- Driving the mother-in-law to appointments so she doesn't have to take the free senior van.
- Cleaning out the mother-in-law's garage and cleaning up her yard.
- Babysitting Danny so he doesn't run away and give Granny her third heart attack.

WHAT DID YOU SAY?

I try to avoid the north hallway after lunch. That's because Nick and his minions gather there every day to exchange vape pods before they hit the bathrooms.

Today, Tom and I have to stop at Ms. Lane's to pick up study guides.

Nick is standing near the lockers outside Ms. Lane's door.

"Hey, Brain Damage, are you trying to dress code Swiss Alps?"

As usual, a nonsense comment.

"Wait, what did you just say?" Ms. Lane steps out and gets close to Nick's face, like so close he can probably smell whatever she just had for lunch.

He freezes. His face turns red. And then he does what would send any teacher over the edge. He smirks.

"What. Did. You. Say?"

"He said something about me dress coding Molly," Tom says.

Ms. Lane takes a deep breath. "Nick, to the office now. *Now.*"

He turns, still smirking, adjusts the red baseball cap sticking out of his back pocket, and saunters toward the office.

"Tom, stay here a second. Molly, can I talk to you?"

We go into her room and close the door. She asks me what he called me. I tell her everything, even why Nick calls me Swiss Alps. I pull out the folded list of Megan Birch nicknames. I tell her about the n-word and mental midget and all the other horrors that spill from Nick's mouth on a daily basis. By the end, she's shaking with rage.

"But why hasn't anyone reported it? At least put a complaint in the Bully Box?"

I roll my eyes. "People have. Nothing ever happens."

"Well, something is going to happen this time. Thank you, Molly. I'll take care of this."

"Okay. But, Ms. Lane, if it means having to drag Tom down to the office to confront Nick, please don't do it. Tom doesn't need that."

She stares at me. "The only one going to the office is Nick."

THE BULLY BOX

There's a wooden box with a slit on top nailed to the wall in the west hallway near the nurse's office. It's officially called a suggestion box, but everyone calls it the Bully Box, because we're supposed to feel comfortable sticking anonymous tips in it when we're being bullied.

People have used the Bully Box in many ways:

- As a curse-word deposit box.
- As a way to get your mortal enemies in trouble by accusing them of being bullies.
- As a way to report teachers for giving too much homework or having coffee breath.
- As a garbage can for gum stuck to scrap paper.

Once, though, when we were in seventh grade, someone actually reported bullying. Within hours, Couchman called the reporter down to the office and interrogated her. She started crying and admitted she was the one who put the note in the Bully Box. Couchman called the bully out of class and made the girl who wrote the note face him. The girl ran out of the school, and her parents flipped out on Couchman.

That started the rumor that the Bully Box wasn't anonymous, that Couchman had cameras watching us, and why should people report bullying anonymously if Couchman was just going to rat out the reporter to the bully?

The parents demanded a meeting and asked for proof that there were no cameras at Fisher. The board of education said it would cost thousands of dollars to install cameras, and our district didn't have thousands of dollars, even if they did want cameras.

After the active-shooter lockdown, the parents had another meeting demanding the district install cameras.

"We don't have thousands of dollars," the board of education said.

Nothing ever happened to the bully, even though the note said this:

Nick held the girls' room door shut and wouldn't let me out until I admitted I was the fattest girl in school.

Now that we know there are no cameras, people have gone back to using the Bully Box for the usual stuff.

The girl who wrote the note transferred to another school.

The bully is still a bully.

We plot our plan to fill the halls with anti-dress-code signs, and our White Dresses group chat turns into Signs for Justice. We meet at my house after school for Thai food and rebel art.

Mom walks in to find us sprawled out on the kitchen floor.

"What are you girls up to?" she asks, picking up a spring roll.

"We're making signs to protest the dress code," I say. "We're hanging them after lacrosse."

"Did you get permission?"

"Not really. But the interim superintendent hasn't done anything with the petition, and nothing is changing. It would be an act of peaceful resistance."

"Well, there you go," Mom says, smiling a little.

We line our signs up in a row on the dining room table, the first good use for the dining room table since Thanksgiving.

o o o

Navya and I carry the signs to lacrosse practice in a brown paper bag stapled shut. The Thai noodles gnaw at my gut as I run up and down the field in the sweltering heat.

"We need to go in to use the bathroom," Navya tells Coach. (It's not really a lie since we do have to go.)

We get into the school, a creepy crypt of a place when nobody's there.

"Ready?" Navya says, ripping open the paper bag.

"Derny, Dern, Dern, what's happening, dude? You want to go hit some balls?"

It's Dr. Couchman, and he's shouting down the east hallway like he's Mr. Dern's frat brother.

"I'm in. Give me a minute to take a leak."

"Gross," I whisper to Navya. We slip into the girls' room and wait.

"We can't take a chance," I say. "We'll ruin the whole thing."

We text, **Plan Aborted.**

And then Pearl has an idea.

∘ ∘ ∘

Every Thursday morning, the community service club meets at seven. Pearl runs the club, and Mr. Henke is always late, so the custodian lets Pearl in before he goes to Dunkin' Donuts for coffee.

Pearl, Olivia, Navya, Bea, and I meet in the woods at six thirty in the morning. Liza can't be here because she takes the bus from Hartford, and we thought it was best if Mary Kate and Lucy stayed away since they still have a year left at this place.

Pearl lets us in the side door near the chorus room at 6:50.

"We have to hurry, like run," Pearl says. "We have ten minutes."

We fan out and sprint, taping three signs each to the walls, using blue painter's tape so we don't ruin the paint. (That was Bea's idea. Her dad is very particular.)

We sprint back to the chorus room, gasping for air, and escape out to the garden at precisely 6:56.

"Well done, team," Pearl says, before disappearing back into the school to await Mr. Henke and the other club members.

The rest of us hang out in the woods, near the grave of the headless bird. We're full of adrenaline and a fair amount of fear.

"What if they have cameras?" Olivia asks.

"They don't," Navya says. "Remember the Bully Box situation?"

"Ah, yes."

Hearts thumping.

Hands sweating.

Minds racing.

We wait for the bell.

RULES FOR GETTING CAUGHT

1. Be brave.
2. If you can take the blame yourself without dragging others down with you, definitely do that.
3. Never apologize.
4. Figure out who your allies are.
5. Record it for later.

SOMETIMES ALL YOU NEED TO KNOW ABOUT SOMEONE IS TUCKED INSIDE A GREEN FOLDER

I'm having a proud moment.

Everybody is talking about our signs.

Two minutes after the first bell rings, Mrs. Peabody calls my name over the loudspeaker. Navya is in my homeroom. She shoots me a please-don't-tell-on-me look. I smile and wink. Of course Couchman assumes I did it. I'm the founder and CEO of *Dress Coded: A Podcast.*

"Have a seat, Molly." Mrs. Peabody points to the wobbly chair outside the meeting room. Somebody scribbled *I love Jim* in black Sharpie on the back of the chair.

For some reason, I'm not scared, not like I would have been if I had been called to the office that first day of seventh grade, when Liza was dress coded. We have only a couple weeks of school left. I wouldn't be devastated if I missed the last lacrosse game (like Navya would). My parents won't punish me. And, most of all, I believe in what we're doing.

I'm calm.

I turn on my phone voice recorder just as the door opens.

"Molly Frost." Dr. Couchman looks down at a piece of paper, probably because he doesn't know who I am and has to read my name. "Come on in."

I sit across from him and our guidance counselor, Ms. Santos-Skinner. She gives me a little wave and a smile. I set the phone down on top of my language arts binder.

"I'm sure you're aware of the posters criticizing our school dress-code policy that mysteriously went up all over the school this morning," Dr. Couchman says.

"You mean criticizing the unfair dress-code policy?" I ask. "Yes."

No stomachache. No sweaty hands. Just calm.

Dr. Couchman looks at Ms. Santos-Skinner and shakes his head.

"Several students came to me to let me know you are doing some kind of anti-dress-code podcast. I'm just going to ask you point-blank: Did you put up the posters?"

I stare at him. "Who were the several students? I have a right to know."

"I'm going to go ahead and keep that confidential."

"Like you kept the Bully Box girl confidential?"

I glance at Ms. Santos-Skinner. Her eyes get wide. I've only seen her a couple of times to talk about my schedule. I have no idea if her eyes are saying *How dare you talk to the principal like that?* or *You go, girl!*

"I'll tell you everything if you tell me who the several students are. Those are my terms."

He stands up and leans over the table, his face scrunched up like a slouch sock. "Do you want to be suspended? Because that's where you're headed."

I definitely don't want to be suspended and risk missing finals, getting incompletes, and ending up back here next year. "Fine. You win. It was me. And I'm not sorry."

"You hung the signs?" Ms. Santos-Skinner asks.

"Yup."

"So you broke into my building, then?" Dr. Couchman asks, still standing.

"I didn't break in. The chorus door was wide open this morning, so I walked in. If there's a rule in the handbook against walking in and hanging signs, I must have missed it. We've been hanging signs about fund-raisers and clubs all year without permission."

"You meant to cause trouble," Dr. Couchman says.

"You definitely don't know what I meant."

"Okay, Molly, what if you agree to take down the signs and set up an appointment to meet with me for a counseling session?" Ms. Santos-Skinner says.

"I'm not comfortable taking down the signs. But I'd be happy to meet to talk about how damaging this dress code is to the female children at your school."

"You better believe we're going to take down the signs—together, right now," Dr. Couchman says. "And you're getting detention for sneaking in and vandalizing our school."

"I didn't sneak in, and posters are not vandalism."

"Let's go." He holds the door for me.

I look back at Ms. Santos-Skinner, who is shaking her head, and again, I don't know if she's shaking her head to say *Dumb girl, causing trouble* or *Dumb principal, misusing the word* vandalism.

I hold the phone in one hand as I walk with Dr. Couchman. At each sign, I read it loudly, then carefully pull it down.

Stop Shaming Girls

Oh No! My Shoulder Is Showing!

Fight Unfair Dress Codes

Stop Staring at Me, You Creepy Old Dude

Why Is My Stomach Skin More Important
Than My Education?

Teach Boys Self-Control!

I Am More Than My Clothing

We miss the two signs on the inside doors of the girls' bathroom stalls. Those are mine. I put them in there on purpose. They both say:

Stand with Us

@DressCodedAPodcast

#DressCoded

"Bye, Dr. Couchman," I say. "Hope you change the handbook."

He mumbles something under his breath and wanders away.

"Oh, do I get to keep my signs? I worked really hard on those," I call out.

If he actually bothered to know any of his students (other than the baseball players), he would know there was no way I could do the beautiful artwork on Bea's sign. But he doesn't know me or Bea.

"No," he calls back.

After school, Ms. Santos-Skinner chases me through the crowd to the bus area and hands me a white trash bag.

"I found this in the recycling bin," she says with a wink.

Mary Kate and I tear open the bag when we get on the bus.

All of our signs are there, neatly stacked inside a green folder.

At least I know where Ms. Santos-Skinner stands.

When I get home, I tell Mom everything.

She already knows. "Yeah, I got a call."

"Are you mad?"

"Not at all." She puts her arm around me and squeezes my shoulder.

I tell her what happened with Dr. Couchman and that detention starts tomorrow, but that people were excited we started the dress-code protest.

"I'll probably have to be there with Nick, who got in trouble for calling me 'Swiss Alps' and Tom 'Brain Damage.'"

"That's horrible. Wait, why 'Swiss Alps'?"

"It's too ridiculous to say." I pivot and eat an orange slice. "Have you heard anything about Danny?"

"He's actually doing well. Granny's cooking him all his favorites, and he's talking to Daddy about real things for once." She laughs. "If somebody told me ten years ago I'd have one kid seeing an addiction doctor and one kid going to detention and I'd be fine with it, I wouldn't have believed them."

"I think Danny is going to be okay, Mom."

She smiles. "Yeah, me too."

Thibodeaux follows me to the tree house, and I hoist him up. I open the green folder and hang our signs on the tree-house wall. Tibby and I lie on the floor and look around. Our tree house has been home to many of my best ideas. Now it's a headquarters. And I have a feeling it will stay this way until that handbook changes or we change.

Or both.

DRESS CODED: A PODCAST

ME: Hello, Fisher Middle School and beyond. My name is Molly Frost, and this is *Dress Coded: A Podcast,* episode six. Today is a special edition of *Dress Coded.* I don't have a guest. Instead, I will play for you the entire conversation that occurred when our school principal called me down to his office for hanging anti-dress-code posters. Enjoy.

I HEAR THE CHEERS

I hear the cheers bouncing off the stop signs and oak trees and woodland creatures scurrying around our town. *Go, Molly Frost. You are fierce, girl.* It's the most popular podcast yet, and I'm full of warm, bright light. I'm as brave as I was when I didn't care what people thought of me.

That was a long time ago.

LETTER TO PARENTS

Dear FMS Parents,

Please continue to encourage your children to follow the code of conduct laid out in our student handbook, specifically with regard to the dress-code policy. I know children can get antsy with the hot weather approaching, but let's save beach attire for the beach.

I would like to take this opportunity to clarify the dress code for our Moving Up Day ceremony on June 15. Boys should wear khaki pants, dress shoes, and a white button-down shirt with a tie. Girls should wear white dresses that fully cover the shoulders and collarbone, and fall at or below the knee. Violations of the dress code on this occasion will result in students being asked to leave. Also, please refrain from flash photography during the ceremony. We look forward to a tasteful and celebratory evening.

Sincerely,
Jim Couchman, EdD

THE SIGNS FOR JUSTICE GROUP CHAT IS NOW BACK TO BEING THE WHITE DRESSES GROUP CHAT (FOR OBVIOUS REASONS)

PEARL: Are you okay, Molly? I'm really sorry you had to go to the office alone.

ME: I'm good. It was actually kind of fun.

NAVYA: You were amazing in there.

ME: Thank you. I felt a little amazing.

OLIVIA: The best part was "posters are not vandalism."

EVERYONE: LOLOLOL

ME: So, how are we addressing the Couchman white dress letter?

BEA: It's going to be a million degrees.

NAVYA: I finally found a dress, and I'm not returning it. I can't believe this.

OLIVIA: Same.

BEA: Same.

LIZA: Dress coded for #collarbone. LOL

ME: LOL

Me in real life: That dress store had a no-return policy. My dress is strapless. It very much shows my shoulders and my collarbone, and it falls above my knee, and I know my parents can't afford another dress.

PEARL: My mom is furious.

LIZA: I'm wearing the dress I have. I don't care if my collarbone and knees show. They can kick me out. I'm sick of this school.

EVERYONE: ME TOO.

NAVYA: Ashley, are you out there? Hello? Ashley?

Ashley never answers.

DETENTION IS ANOTHER WORD FOR "MY WORST NIGHTMARE COME TRUE"

I'm stuck having an awkward conversation with Mr. Dern, who tells everyone he gets paid extra to oversee detention because he's saving up for a Range Rover someday.

"Dress-Code Girl," he says, "I'm guessing it's time to stop all this nonsense. You don't want to get a reputation in high school."

"What does that mean?"

"You know what that means."

Nick comes bouncing in and stops dead in his tracks when he sees me. "Why is she here? Oh, wait, I know why."

"Were you one of the unidentified snitches who turned me in? Or were you the only snitch who turned me in?"

"It's your fault I'm here," he says.

I don't have any interest in arguing with him.

I sit as close to the window as I can without crawling out and stare at the Kindness Garden.

Whoever invented the phrase *choose kindness* was probably not sitting in a classroom with Mr. Dern and Nick.

Dern's phone starts blasting a country music song, and he jumps up to answer it outside. "Dude, you want to drive to Fenway tonight? I just scored two tickets from my golf buddy." The door clicks shut, and I can hear his muffled high-pitched laughter coming from out in the garden.

I'm alone in a room with Nick. I'm fully expecting his Swiss Alps or Snot Drop taunts to start up. Maybe he'll even invent a new one now that he has a little time to relax and reflect. But he doesn't say a word. He hunches over the desk and pretends to be reading the book *Ghost*, about the kid on the running team. I know he's pretending, because *Ghost* is a page-turner and he hasn't turned the page in seven minutes.

I stare at the clock on the wall above Dern's desk, watching the second hand move around and around. One of Nick's hands lies flat on the desk, his other hand fidgets with the corner of the page, and he keeps his eyes down.

"What time is this over?" I finally ask. I can't deal with the weirdness in the room.

He keeps his eyes glued to the page. "Three," he mumbles.

And it all clicks.

Nick needs his groupies. Without his groupies, he can't be brave. He can't be a bully. He can't be anything but a twitchy little boy fake-reading in an empty classroom with a girl who is beginning to learn she has no more patience for twitchy little boys like him.

Like Couchman.

Like Dern.

Like her own brother.

BEAR STICKS

When I get out to the garden, the mom of Violeta, the FMS grad who died in Iraq, is kneeling on a little stool and digging under a rosebush.

"Hello," I say, trying not to startle her. She squints up at me, and I move so the sun isn't in her eyes. "I just wanted to tell you the stuff you said about your daughter at the Memorial Day ceremony was beautiful. She sounded like an awesome person."

She smiles. "Yes, she was an awesome person." She stands up and wipes her hands on her pants. "You're a student here?"

"Yeah. I kind of sort of had detention today."

"Detention? What kinds of things get kids detention these days?"

"Well, I put up a bunch of signs protesting our unfair dress code."

"That's it?"

"Yeah. The girls at Fisher are constantly getting harassed about wearing tank tops, shorts—pretty much anything normal people wear."

She shakes her head. "Wow."

I realize I'm complaining about dress codes to a lady who

has to deal with much more horrible things. "I'm sorry for talking about this. I mean, after what you've been through."

"No, no. Don't you be sorry. I can tell you Violeta would have been in detention with you, no doubt in my mind. I bet she's smiling down on you right now."

"Really?"

"Oh, she was all about justice. Do you know how much garbage she got being a female in the military?"

Violeta's mom bends down and picks up a kindness rock that has somehow made its way to the edge of the rosebushes. She holds it up and shows me; it says *YOU'VE GOT THIS* in bold red letters. "See, I bet that's Violeta sending you a message, kiddo."

I take the rock and slide it into my backpack pocket. "Thanks, Violeta," I say, looking up at the flat rays streaming through a storm cloud.

"Have you taken this up with the board of education? I know a couple of the members. They may be willing to look over the dress-code policy."

"We've sent a petition to the interim superintendent, but we haven't tried the board yet. My friend did a few years ago, and nothing happened."

"There are new members now. I would try to get on the agenda for next week's meeting. It can't hurt."

"You're right. Thank you. It can't hurt." I pick up my backpack and brush the dirt off the bottom. "I better get home."

"You're going into the woods? There are bears in there."

"I'm used to them. We pretty much avoid each other."

"Oh, no. I'm gonna walk with you. That mama bear could charge you if her cubs are around."

"She knows me."

"I don't care if she knows you. She's four hundred pounds."

Violeta's mom searches the woodpile between the garden and the woods for a big stick. She pulls another stick out of the pile for me. "Here. Carry this, just in case."

I convince her she needs to walk me only halfway, and she watches until I get to the edge of Will's yard. I guess when you lose a daughter, it's hard not to worry about other people's daughters.

I lean my bear stick against our tree-house tree and wonder if the bears tell their kids to watch out for us.

WHAT MATTERS TO ASHLEY'S MOM

Ashley cancels our double sleepover two and a half hours before I'm supposed to be at her house. It doesn't matter that Mom is packed for Granny's, or that she filled a bag with Ashley's favorite snacks. It doesn't matter that I've been hoping for this chance to talk about how we've barely talked since I started the podcast. What matters is that I know Ashley's mom isn't "under the weather," like she texted Mom, and that she doesn't "have to postpone" so she doesn't "get Molly sick for all the end-of-the-year festivities."

She's canceling because she doesn't want Ashley hanging out with the kid whose brother is the town nicotine dealer. That looks bad.

Ashley's mom doesn't want to be associated with anything that looks bad.

Ashley texts me a bunch of times.

ASHLEY: Are you mad at me?

ASHLEY: Sorry, my mom is a hypochondriac.

ASHLEY: Maybe we could hang
out Sunday?

ME: It's fine, Ash.

I want to talk about Ashley behind her back and complain about how her mom is mean to the guy who mows their lawn and once refused to give a kid candy on Halloween because he was wearing a Barack Obama costume. But complaining about Ashley's mom would make me just as rude as she is. And complaining about Ashley would mean admitting our friendship is even sicker than her mom is pretending to be.

I tear open the bag of salt-and-vinegar chips Mom bought because she knows they're Ashley's favorite.

And then I have an idea.

ME: Hey, Megan. I know this is going
to sound weird, and you don't have
to say yes, but my parents have to
go away this weekend and Ashley
canceled our sleepover because her
mom's sick. I'm wondering if your
parents would let me crash at your
house until Sunday?

MEGAN: Why is that weird?

ME: I don't know.

MEGAN: Yeah, come over.
We're ordering Chinese in a few
minutes. Text me your order.

ME: Okay. I'll be there in a
little while.

IT'S HARD TO CALL ADULTS ON THE PHONE AND ACT PROFESSIONAL

I look up the district office number on the school website and call the interim superintendent's secretary, Mary Lou Louis.

"Um, hello. My name is Molly Frost, and I'm wondering how to get something on the next board meeting agenda."

Pause.

"What is it you would like to get on the agenda?"

"Changing the Fisher Middle School dress code in the handbook."

Pause.

"Are you the one with the petition?"

"Well, yeah, it's my friends and me. By the way, has he had a chance to look at it?"

"I'll have to get back to you."

Double pause.

"So it looks like the agenda for next Friday is full. We have bear hunting and artificial turf."

"Bear hunting?" I'm shocked.

"Yes, people are afraid the bears are going to kill somebody."

"They're not."

"So I would recommend tabling your topic for the start of next year."

"Okay." I'm just about to hang up. "Is there anything we can do to get on the agenda?"

"There's usually time allotted for public comment at the end of each meeting. You may have an opportunity go up to the mic and say a few words, depending on how long the meeting goes."

"Thank you."

"Good luck."

I need to warn the bears about this meeting.

GOOD GHOSTS

Mom drops me off at Megan's and stays a few minutes to make sure her parents don't seem like serial killers. Dr. and Dr. Birch (now I get why Megan is so good at science) are on their giant front porch drinking tea and reading, which to Mom means: *Yup. Not serial killers.*

Mom is grateful somebody is willing to take her kid so she can go visit Dad and Danny and Granny and Granny's cat, Alph (although I'm sure Mom isn't thinking about Alph). Megan is excited to show me around their farm-house, which is way up on the outskirts of town, between the apple orchards and the farm everybody visits to learn about animals and buy fresh eggs.

"I love your house," I say, staring at all the interesting artwork on the living room wall. There's a giant painting of a hot-air balloon over the fireplace. It makes me happy.

"Thank you." She leads me up a staircase. "I'm pretty sure it's haunted, but they're good ghosts."

"How do you know they're good ghosts?"

"I just know."

Megan's room has yellow walls and soft white bedding and rows of Polaroid pictures. "You and Graham go on trips together?" I ask, pointing at a picture of them on a beach.

"Every year, our families go away the last week of summer vacation. That was Aruba."

"Wow."

We hike through the orchards and wander around Graham's family's farm. Graham comes riding out of the barn on a chestnut-colored horse.

"Hey, G. Say hi to Molly."

"Howdy." He tips his baseball cap.

"I started riding when I was three," Megan says. "You know, with the CP, it felt good to be riding, because walking was a little challenging."

"Do you have your own horse?"

She nods. "Millie is at a barn up the road. We can visit her tomorrow if you want."

Nothing is stressful at Megan's house. Her parents cook together. Graham comes in and out, looking for snacks or hanging out on the couch. Her dogs are snuggly. Her older sister is friendly. Even the ghosts are nice. It's warm, safe, comfortable, and fun. I love my own family, but I don't want to leave Birch Farm.

I don't even care one bit that Ashley forgets her mom's lie and posts a picture on Snapchat of herself at the mall (with her mom in the background).

Horses. Hot-air balloons. Fresh scrambled eggs and a picture of Megan and me wearing clay face masks taped to her lemon-yellow wall. That's all that matters right now.

We go from lab partners to double-sleepover friends in one weekend. It's the best weekend I've had in a long, long time.

"Megan, can I ask you something?" I say as I slide under the white comforter, right before sleep.

"Yeah."

"You know that list of names you showed me in science class? How are you still happy? How has all that horrible stuff not affected you?"

"My mom always says, 'Don't give them your energy.' Because while energy is neither created nor destroyed, it can be transferred. She tells me that when they say awful things, it bounces off of me, and all the negative energy goes right back into the Nicks of the world. It's simple physics."

"And that works?"

"Yep. It actually works."

According to Megan, it's hard to argue with physics.

SINCE TIME BEGAN, HIGH SCHOOL GIRLS HAVE TRIED TO MAKE MIDDLE SCHOOL GIRLS FEEL COMFORTABLE BY TELLING THEM THEY ARE GORGEOUS (IT USUALLY WORKS)

I get to enjoy detention with Nick, Mr. Dern, a girl named Louise who punches people to be funny (but ends up leaving bruises), and eight seventh-grade boys who were caught vaping in Mr. Lu's supply closet.

I find out we're allowed to listen to music, which changes everything. It's just me, my math homework, and Dad's classic Rolling Stones mix blocking everything out until three o'clock, when I rush out and find Liza, who missed the bus.

"What's detention like?" Liza asks as we're walking through the garden toward the woods.

"It's the feeling you get when you step in gum, run into a glass door, spill an entire container of yogurt on the floor, and find hair in your food all at the same time."

"Hmm. Sounds fun."

Mom's still on her way home from Granny's. She wanted to go to Danny's addiction doctor appointment, so I went straight from Megan's to Will's to school.

At my house, Liza and I forage for food and find three peanut butter energy bars, two bananas, and water. I still remember Liza telling me my house smelled like snacks. It must not even smell like snacks these days.

"Tree house?" I ask.

"Most definitely."

We wait on the back deck for Mama Bear and her cubs to slowly wander through our yard. Liza takes a hundred pictures, and her mom calls to scream at her to get into the house. The bears haven't made it to the middle of Hartford. Yet.

"Are they going to eat me?" Liza asks.

"No. They prefer bird feeders and trash cans." I watch them disappear into the woods behind Will's. "Don't worry, we have a bear stick if we need one." I point to the stick leaning against the tree. Liza sprints toward the tree house and grabs it.

"Welcome to headquarters," I announce when we crawl through the hatch.

"Our posters look so good." Liza has spent more time here than anyone except Will and me. "This moving-up ceremony thing is making me want to wear the most inappropriate thing I can find."

"Right? It's infuriating."

Liza shakes her head. "We're going to wear what we're going to wear. And I pray we get kicked out. When my brother graduated from Fisher, Couchman spent twenty minutes rambling about how baseball is a metaphor for life. It was torture."

We listen to the podcast of me standing up to Dr. Couchman in the office. Because of me, everybody now has to leave their phones in a pouch attached to a hook above the I-love-Jim chair before they go in to see Couchman. Also because of me, @DressCodedAPodcast has gotten pretty popular.

Jessica, the senior, and her friend show up at the tree house a few minutes before four.

"Remember Jasmine?" Jessica asks.

"Hey, girls. Nice to see you." If Jasmine were an animal, she'd be part puppy, part bunny, and part hummingbird.

"You're really pretty," Liza says.

"Thank you. So are you," Jasmine says. "Wow. You're both gorgeous."

Liza and Jessica sit against the wall and wait for Jasmine to tell her story.

"Tell Danny I said hi." Jasmine smiles. "He was my very first fake boyfriend."

"Really? I had no idea Danny had girlfriends, even fake ones."

She laughs. "It was third grade, and he brought me pudding soup. He poured chocolate milk into chocolate pudding and stirred it, and then gave it to me in a Thomas the Tank Engine thermos. It was delicious."

"Wow. My brother never ceases to amaze me."

"He's a good kid."

Danny never made *me* pudding soup.

DRESS CODED: A PODCAST

ME: Hello, Fisher Middle School and beyond. My name is Molly Frost, and this is *Dress Coded: A Podcast*, episode seven. So, Jasmine, can you tell us a little about yourself?

JASMINE: I row crew, and I hang out with the crew team. I'm going to UCLA next year, and I'm planning to be an environmental lawyer. And I'm really hoping to learn how to surf. My boyfriend is going to UConn. He got into the honors program. I don't know. That's about it.

ME: That's great. So were you dress coded at Fisher Middle?

JASMINE: *[Laughs.]* Every other day. Fingertip started in right away, and nobody knew what to wear. We had bought all these clothes, and our parents were really annoyed that we couldn't wear most of them.

ME: Did your parents say anything?

JASMINE: They just complained about wasting all their money on clothes we couldn't wear. They pretty much took it out on us.

Liza blurts out, *"Yup!"*

ME: Was there a specific incident you want to tell us about?

JASMINE: A few days before the end of the school year, I went to the shore with my friends and got a really bad sunburn on my shoulders and chest. It was so painful I couldn't sleep. I had to take Advil, and anyway, it was torture. It hurt so bad I had to walk around in a tube top. That Monday, I went to school in a tank top. The sunburn was still itchy and excruciating.

ME: That's awful.

JASMINE: Yeah. It was. Wear your sunscreen, kids. This is hard to say, because it was so embarrassing, but I was sitting in first-period language arts, and Dr. Couchman stuck his head in and asked me to go with him to the office. I still remember he walked ahead of me and didn't talk to me the whole way there. And when we got to his office, he closed the door and . . . ugh.

Her eyes fill with tears, and Jessica sits on the floor in front of her and holds her hands.

JASMINE: He pretended to be reading something until Fingertip came in. She looked at me like I was the most vile creature on earth and asked me why I wasn't wearing a bra. Couchman just sat there holding his stupid laminated dress code.

"No," Liza yells out. "That is not okay."

JASMINE: I was shocked. I didn't know what to do. I just mumbled something about having a sunburn and the straps were too painful. Fingertip said I was violating the dress code as it was, by wearing a tank top, but that

going without a bra was grossly inappropriate and my
parents would have to bring me a bra or take me home.

ME: Oh, Jasmine. I'm so sorry they did that to you.

I don't have to ask her how that made her feel. We all
know how that made her feel. Like a tiny bug flicked away.
Like a bug squished on the floor. Like a braless bug.

JASMINE: I remember hunching my shoulders, shrinking
into the chair because I was so humiliated. I left his office
and started to cry on the phone with my mom, and Mrs.
Peabody kept saying "There, there," and I felt like that
was such a dumb thing to say to someone. My mom
picked me up and let me stay home until the sunburn
felt better. I still had to go to school the last day to clean
out my locker and everything. I was terrified to run into
Fingertip or Couchman.

ME: Did your mom say anything to the school?

JASMINE: No. But she took me for a manicure and let me
watch as much TV as I wanted. And she let me skip the
moving-up ceremony. I was grateful for that, but . . .

ME: But what?

JASMINE: I started staying home more and more. I was so
stressed-out about how I looked all the time. I mean, I
was stressed-out before the dress coding, but it got so
much worse after. It took me a really long time to feel
okay in my own skin. I still have trouble with that.

ME: But you're so beautiful.

JASMINE: People say that, and I appreciate it, really. But I guess it's hard to stop picking myself apart and focusing on the things I hate about myself. Anyway, I'll never forget what they did to me in that office. I don't want anyone to ever feel that way again.

ME: Thank you for sharing your story, Jasmine.

JASMINE: Thank you for doing this, Molly.

Rage and shame have set our headquarters on fire. It is all ablaze. There are pieces of Jasmine's soul in the bits of ash that fly through the air. Pieces of all of our souls.

When ash falls to the ground, it grows gardens.

GOALS

Liza goes with me to the last lacrosse game of middle school. She carries the bear stick, and I wonder if Violeta's mom should start an actual bear-stick business.

"I miss the tree house," Liza says. "We used to have so much fun."

"I know. That was the best summer. Remember the night it poured, and we chased that slimy frog for, like, two hours?"

"I totally forgot about Froggy McSlippman. We never did catch him."

"Let's try to see each other more this summer."

"Yes. I miss my Molly. I even miss Will, my archenemy."

"He never hated you. He was just jealous."

"I get it. I stole you."

"Our little Will is starting to like girls. It's very sweet."

"It happens to the best of them."

Mom shows up just as the game starts. She sits with Navya's mom, which is the same as sitting alone, because Navya's mom cannot resist yelling and screaming the entire game. Navya's used to it by now.

I don't know if it's because I'm still full of rage from Jasmine's interview, or because it's unseasonably cool and I can run better, or just luck, but I play my best game ever.

Mom even stands up and cheers a few times, and Mom hates sports.

Navya sees me ripping up the field and glances back. It's almost as if time slows down. My friend fights every ounce of her own instinct to barrel toward the goal herself so she can give her former backyard student a chance. She hurls it. I catch it (miracle number one) and cut right, surprising the Taft Middle School girl in front of me, and then, without really thinking, I shoot. And I score (miracle number two).

We don't win, and Navya wears her sad duck face all the way to the Mexican restaurant, but I've made the first goal of my lacrosse career.

Liza eats guacamole with us. Her mom shows up and squeezes in next to me, and Liza starts telling our moms about Jasmine's podcast.

They listen, wide-eyed.

"I had no idea it was this bad." Navya's mom shakes her head. "Thank goodness you girls are out of there."

I stare down at the pile of chips on my plate.

"So, what? We just leave and go back in a few years when some other eighth grader starts a podcast?" Liza says. "It's not right."

"Have you heard anything about the petition you sent the interim superintendent?" Mom asks, reaching her arm up to signal for more guacamole.

Navya and I shake our heads.

"You should take it up with the board of ed," Navya's mom says. "They might be willing to change the hand-book."

"I tried that." I take a sip of lemonade. "They said we

have to wait until next year to get on the agenda, but we can speak if there's time at the end of the meeting."

"Do you want *me* to call and see if I can get you some time?" Navya's mom asks.

I nod. "It can't hurt."

(Or can it?)

Our moms talk in hushed voices, but we know they're talking about us and Dr. Couchman and the dress code. I hope they're talking about why, up until now, they haven't said or done anything to make things easier for all the daughters at Fisher Middle School.

A DIFFERENT AGENDA

Navya and her mom try to get the dress-code issue at Fisher Middle School added to the last board meeting of the school year. The secretary tells Navya's mom exactly what she told me: There's no room on the agenda because they have to debate whether or not to put in a crumb-rubber sports field. Then they have to talk about the pros and cons of murdering bears on school property.

"You can't spare five minutes just to hear these girls out?" Navya's mom says.

"No, sorry. They'll have to try to get in a comment at the end or wait to be on the agenda next year."

Suddenly, the camping trip chaperones want twenty-five dollars per kid to buy food and other supplies. This gets parents complaining, and then the chaperones complain they're the ones doing all the heavy lifting (whatever that means). And of course all the parent drama rubs off on their kids.

> **JACK:** None of this would have happened if Olivia hadn't ruined the school camping trip.

> **RAHUL:** This has nothing to do with Olivia.

> **JACK:** Of course it does.

> **EMMA:** Couchman would have found an excuse to cancel the trip and you know it.

> **NICK:** It's Olivia's fault. Tampon fail.

Two hundred seventeen drops to 216. I text Olivia.

> **ME:** You okay?

OLIVIA: Yeah.

> **ME:** Want to meet me after
> detention Thursday? Fruit
> Roll-Ups?

Olivia and I ate Fruit Roll-Ups for snack nearly every day of fifth grade.

OLIVIA: Sure.

GUTS ARE GROSS. WHY SHOULD WE BE TRUSTING THEM?

Mom texts me in the middle of language arts to tell me there's been another school shooting in a town just like ours: **Molly, please know how much I love you, and remember, if this ever happens at your school, stay present and listen to your gut. Be safe. Love you.**

Five minutes later, I get a text from Dad: **Just wanted to let you know I'm thinking about you, Molls. Hope all is well. Back soon. I love you.**

I'm not the only one getting parent love texts.

After a while, Ms. Lane makes us turn our phones off.

All the love is getting distracting.

At lunch, everyone's talking about the camping trip. It's four days away, and some parents are threatening to take their kids out because "twenty-five dollars is steep." Mom agrees it's steep, but she wants me to have a good time before Danny gets back Sunday.

"It's not that expensive," Ashley says. "It's like the cost of a breakfast at Starbucks."

Navya looks at Ashley. "You know there are people who don't eat breakfast at Starbucks practically every day, right? And there are people who might find it pretty expensive to buy sleeping bags, flashlights, and all the other stuff you need for camping. Duh, Ash."

"I really don't think Fisher Middle School people are that strapped for cash," Ashley says.

We all stare at her in disbelief.

"I'm just using my own money," Bea says. "My parents don't want me to go to this thing anyway. They'll totally keep me home and act like it's too expensive."

"Why don't they want you to go?" Navya asks.

"They're afraid I'm going to vape, or kiss somebody or something."

"You're not going to vape, but you never know about

the other thing," Navya says, raising her eyebrows. "You're getting those braces off today."

"I think I'll give my mouth a chance to relax before it meets somebody else's mouth," Bea says.

"What are we talking about?" Tom hardly ever talks. Sometimes we forget he's here.

"The camping trip," I say.

"What camping trip?"

I've found the one kid not in our original 217-person group chat.

"Our class is going camping this weekend," Bea says. "You should come."

Tom furrows his eyebrows, and I can't tell if he's confused or hurt. "Yeah. That would be fun." He bites into his sandwich.

Bea and Navya look at me.

"Do you want to go, Tom? You can come with us," Navya says. "I mean, you can't stay in our tent, but you can hang out with us."

"I have to ask my mom."

I throw out half my lunch and run around the cafeteria looking for Will.

"What's wrong?" he asks.

"Nothing. Listen, would you be willing to share a tent with Tom? Nobody even told him about the camping trip, and I feel bad."

"I'm sharing with Clay and Chen."

"Can you squeeze one more in?"

"How about I don't go because I hate camping?"

"You're going."

"Fine. I'll tell Chen to bring the big tent."

"I love you."

"If you loved me, you'd talk to Pearl."

If I love you, I'll never, ever tell you that Pearl doesn't want anything to do with you.

"I'm planning to do that when we're camping."

"You better."

THE LETTER I WOULD NEVER SEND, BECAUSE I'M NOT CRUEL

Dear Tom,

You will be the only kid in third grade who invites the whole class to your birthday party at the bouncy-house place near the mall and has every single kid RSVP yes. That's because you are cool (as cool as a third grader can be). You can kick the soccer ball really far. You know all about elephants and pelicans. You keep Band-Aids in your desk in case anyone needs one (because you always seem to need one). And the teacher gives you a whole week of free homework passes because you found Myrtle the class turtle (has any class turtle ever not been named Myrtle?).

Third grade will be amazing for you, Tom. And then something really bad will happen. You'll go skiing in Vermont over Martin Luther King Day weekend, and you will spin out of control and hit your head on a rock. You will be asleep in the hospital for seven weeks, and when you wake up, you won't be able to walk or feed yourself. You'll work so hard every day to relearn everything. Well, almost everything. You'll never relearn how to be cool.

Ten months after your accident, you'll invite the whole class to your birthday party. Your parents will rent out a movie theater and buy bushels of popcorn and buckets of soda.

Only two kids will show up.

They say TBI stands for "traumatic brain injury." It also stands for "Tom became invisible."

KIDS, THOSE ACROSTIC POEMS YOU LEARN TO WRITE IN SECOND GRADE MIGHT COME IN HANDY SOMEDAY

Mom asks me if I need help studying for exams before she leaves for a lecture at the library on how guinea fowl and possums are better than chemicals for managing ticks. When I got home from detention, she had fresh-baked sourdough bread and assorted cheeses with fig spread waiting for me. Since Dad and Danny left, Mom has been humming and baking and talking to her anti-vaping-advocacy friends and weeding the flowers and playing tug-o'-war with Tibby.

Maybe one bad apple really does spoil the bunch.

I take my bread, cheese, fig spread, and iced tea up to the tree house and organize all my folders and binders. Megan gets dropped off at five, and we struggle to get her up the ladder. She laughs, which makes me laugh, and Tibby stands on the grass whining, because he wants to come up too.

"This is amazing," she says, looking around the headquarters. "I want to make a poster."

"Go for it." I pull out a plastic bin of paper and markers. She works while I try to figure out what I still don't understand from the science review sheets.

"There," she says, eating a chunk of cheddar. "How's this?"

S	TOP
H	ARASSING,
A	NNOYING,
M	OCKING,
E	MBARRASSING
F	EMALES,
U	
L	OUDMOUTH

"It's perfect."

"Too harsh?"

"Not even close."

∘ ∘ ∘

I stay up way too late studying, and wake up exhausted and cranky. Mom drops me off just as the bell is ringing, and I sprint to my locker to grab my lucky number-two pencil, the one with the panda eraser.

"Whoa, whoa, whoa." I hear a familiar voice behind me. "I'd think by the last week of school you'd know better than to show up wearing that."

Fingertip is staring at me like I'm a fly in her soup.

I don't even remember what I'm wearing. I've been deliberately violating the dress code for weeks, and nobody has said anything. *I don't get dress coded. I'm one of the invisibles.*

"I'm sorry. It won't happen again." After all the things I planned to say in this moment, I see no other option but to apologize. I'm about to be late for my final.

"Come on. Down to the office."

"Please"—I realize I don't know her real name—"ma'am. I can't miss my final. I'm really sorry."

She rolls her eyes. "You kids are driving me bonkers. Have some self-respect. Here." She takes off the infamous burgundy cardigan sweater and hands it to me. "Bring it to me at the end of the day. And you're welcome."

My stomach hurts. It's the worst kind of stomachache. The one that comes from a lethal shot of rage and humiliation. "Thank you."

She watches me to make sure I'm putting on her giant cat-hair-covered old-lady sweater that smells of cigarettes and rotting fruit. I run down the hall, clutching my stomach, and slide into my seat just as Mr. Lu is handing out tests.

Megan looks at my burgundy-colored face and matching cardigan sweater and gives me a look that says, *What is happening?* I shake my head and stare down at the blank test paper.

I never got my lucky number-two pencil with the panda eraser.

I'm hot, itchy, disgusted, sick to my stomach, and luckless.

But I finally got dress coded (when I wasn't even trying).

Too bad it's too late to do anything about it.

THINGS GREAT TEACHERS SAY
IN THE HALLWAYS BETWEEN CLASSES

- I heard you had a fantastic game last night.
- I wouldn't doubt that I'll see your name on a Nobel Prize list someday.
- Please, please submit more poems to the literary magazine.
- Hey, can you design the cover for our moving-up ceremony program?
- You've worked so hard this year. I just wanted to let you know I noticed and I'm proud of you.
- Thank you for helping out that new student. She won't forget that.
- I know you're going through a tough time. My classroom is always open if you would like to talk.

WHAT GREAT TEACHERS MEAN
WHEN THEY SAY THOSE THINGS

- You're hard working.
- You're brilliant.
- You're creative.
- You're talented.
- You're not a distraction.
- You're kind.
- You're human.

I don't know what I'm expecting from my last day of detention. Mr. Dern isn't going to greet me with a Frappuccino and a certificate that says:

> I HEREBY AWARD DRESS CODE GIRL,
> SCHOOL VANDAL, WITH A CERTIFICATE
> OF DETENTION COMPLETION.

Olivia and Pearl walk with me to Dern's room. We're planning to go to the store across from the gas station after, for Fruit Roll-Ups. It's weird to think one bad incident has reconnected us all. I'm glad to have them back.

"Are we allowed to bring people to detention if they promise not to talk?" I ask Mr. Dern. It hits me that I never told Olivia that Mr. Dern was in charge of detention and that maybe she doesn't want to spend an hour staring at the guy who started all of this.

"No. That's ridiculous," he says, opening his newspaper to the sports page.

"I'll meet you in the garden in an hour," I tell them. A few minutes later, I see them out on the bench next to the lilac tree.

Nick's gone. It's just me, the seventh-grade vapers, who are all playing games on their phones, and a seventh-grade girl named Talia, from our bus. She moved here midyear from Trinidad. It took Mary Kate and me a while to find Trinidad on the map in my world history textbook.

"Hi, Talia. Why are you here?"

Talia hardly ever talks. I don't even remember what her voice sounds like.

"I talked back to Mr. Buechler in chorus."

"Really?"

She plops down on a chair and fans herself with her glossy ice cream cone folder. "I was really aggravated."

"What happened?"

Dern has his headphones on and is tapping his feet to some middle-aged song that probably reminds him of his glory days.

She whispers, "Is it dress coding if you get sent to the office for having tall hair?"

She tells me the story. I can't even believe what she's saying. I ask her if she'll come to headquarters to tell it again for a podcast.

"If you think it will help," she says.

I don't know if it will help. But people need to know what's happening at this school.

"Can I hug you, Talia?"

She seems surprised. "Yeah."

I scoot my chair over and wrap my arms around her and hug her hard.

It's like a tiny piece of her soul is sticking out, and I'm trying to hug it back in.

I sit on the bench with Olivia and Pearl. They give me a bag of Fruit Roll-Ups.

"Aww. You went to the store for me?"

"It was the least we could do," Olivia says.

I tell them about Talia.

"I'm so mad I can't even see straight," Pearl says. "None of this is okay."

"It's almost over," Olivia says.

"Not for Talia," I say. "And for Mary Kate and Lucy, and all the other seventh graders."

I peel the fruity substance off the plastic, roll it into a ball, and pop it in my mouth. The bees buzz around us, and a giant butterfly lands on the rosebush a few feet away. "It's nice here," I say. They nod.

We look at the White Dresses group chat. Everyone's talking about the camping trip. Ashley and Navya are already packing. The bus leaves from the library parking lot at eleven Saturday morning. Bea sends pictures of her newly straightened teeth. **Gorgeous**, we all text.

Pearl texts, **I'm next**.

Then a new, metal-free era will begin.

Mrs. Tucker comes around the corner with a group of sixth graders. I almost forgot about the Tucker Tours, a tradition where Mrs. Tucker brings groups of sixth graders on a tour of the middle school. After the tour, Mrs. Tucker takes them back to her classroom, where they make their own trail mix and create their official class playlist for seventh grade.

"Our Tucker Tour seems like a century ago," Pearl says.

We watch the sixth graders fan out across the garden in groups of twos and threes. One kid wanders around by himself. Mrs. Tucker waves us over. We stuff the Fruit Roll-Up wrappers in the bag and reluctantly walk over to the piles of kindness rocks.

"Would you girls like to tell our visitors about the Kindness Garden?" she asks, adjusting her tiny-kindness-rock necklace.

I don't think Mrs. Tucker has a clue what happened to Olivia, or what happens to any of the girls at Fisher Middle School. She's great, but she's living in Kindness Rock Land.

Olivia looks at me. "So on the first day of school, you get to bring in a rock. Then you paint an inspirational word or quote that you're supposed to carry with you through middle school."

Mrs. Tucker is beaming with joy. "Pretty neat, huh?"

"I know what I'm going to write," a girl says. "Should I say it, or is it a secret?"

"Go for it," Mrs. Tucker says.

"You rock."

"That is perfect." Mrs. Tucker gives her a high five.

"Another super-creative one," I whisper to Pearl. She laughs.

The kids start yelling out their favorite sayings and running around the garden, smelling roses and chasing butter-flies and pushing each other. Olivia gets quiet. She sits on the bench and rests her elbows on her knees. Tears fall onto the grass.

"What's wrong?" Pearl asks, putting her arm around Olivia.

"They're so excited to come here. It's like they have no idea what's in front of them. How stressful it is to have to look a certain way and dress a certain way, on top of all the other drama." She wipes her eyes. "I just feel bad. They're so . . . happy."

There's nothing I can say to make Olivia feel better.

She's right.

Olivia's dad pulls up. "See you tomorrow," she says.

Pearl and I watch the sixth graders follow Mrs. Tucker to their trail mix and the grand tour of Fisher Middle School.

"Hey, Pearl, any chance you changed your mind about Will? He's kind of still in the middle of his Pearl crush."

She sort of smiles. "He's so sweet. I get what he's feeling. But I'm still in the middle of my secret crush. So no. Please tell him it's not him."

"Still not going to tell me who it is?"

"I've only told Olivia, and you know this person well, so I'm scared to tell you."

"I get it." I'm trying to remember who I know really well.

"Fine. I'm just going to tell you. It's Bea."

I did not see that coming. But then Pearl is kind of artsy in a writer way, and Bea is artsy in a painter way, so they have that in common, but yeah, didn't see it coming.

"Wow. Well, Bea is adorable. That's for sure."

"I like her energy. And her smile. And her art. And she's just an amazing person." She looks at me the exact same way Will looked at me when he was pouring his guts out about her.

"Have you come out? Like, officially?" I ask. "We haven't really hung out this year, so I didn't realize."

"I mean, it's not a secret. A bunch of my friends know. And my family." She laughs. "My grandpa put a rainbow sticker on his phone case, so it's all good. I just haven't told anyone about Bea, except Olivia."

"What should I tell Will?" I ask.

"You can tell him about Bea if you want. I feel bad. I really like Will—as a friend." She bends down and picks up a kindness rock and holds it up. It says *Smile* in electric-blue cursive handwriting.

Pearl looks at me. "Do you think . . . With Bea, do you think there's a chance?"

I can't tell her about the conversation I had with Bea and Navya on the second night of a double sleepover the weekend before Thanksgiving, where Bea said she could see herself dating a girl, but nobody specifically. It's kind of bizarre how it never came up again, and now I'm wondering if I should say something or wait for Bea to bring it up.

I tell Pearl the truth. "I honestly don't know."

DRESS CODED: A PODCAST

ME: Hello, Fisher Middle School and beyond. My name is Molly Frost, and this is *Dress Coded: A Podcast*, episode eight. Today, I'm talking to Talia F., seventh grader and member of Select Choir and the community service club.

Talia motions for me to pause and tells me she can stay only for an hour, because she's meeting her friends at the diner.

ME: So, Talia, can you tell us something about yourself?

TALIA: Uh, okay. This is kind of random, but I help my mom make gigantic batches of chili once a week for homebound veterans. We just finished delivering before I came here.

ME: What do you mean by homebound?

TALIA: They're elderly, and a lot of them are disabled, so they can't leave their houses.

ME: That's really nice of you.

TALIA: We do it through my mom's work. And the other thing I love to do is sing. I'm going to be a professional opera singer.

ME: Do you want to sing something right now?

TALIA: No, thanks.

ME: Okay, so what happened this week to get you detention?

TALIA: It was so frustrating. We were rehearsing for the moving-up ceremony, and I was in front of Josh Morris. In the middle of the song, he started harassing me about my hair.

ME: What's wrong with your hair?

TALIA: I let it go natural, and it's apparently too puffy for Josh, because he wouldn't stop trying to push it down. So I turned around and told him to get his hands off my head. Mr. Buechler stopped everyone and asked what was going on, and Josh said he couldn't see because my hair was in the way. I told him Josh was pushing my hair and that he should keep his hands to himself.

ME: Ugh. That's so frustrating. So why are *you* in detention?

TALIA: Mr. Buechler told me to go to the bathroom and do something with my hair. I told him my hair wasn't the problem. He said he didn't like my attitude and sent me to the office. Dr. Couchman didn't even talk to me. He just came out and told me I had detention, but I'm really lucky I only have to do one day.

She smiles.

I've seen that smile a lot these days. It's easier to smile than to throw a desk through a window.

ME: I'm so sorry, Talia.

TALIA: I can't believe I have to deal with this for another year.

ME: Hopefully not. Listeners, if you want to help us get rid of the Fisher Middle School dress code and speak out about what happened to Talia, please go to the board of ed meeting. We need to stop this.

After Talia tells her story, she makes a sign, and I take a picture of her holding it and post it on our Instagram page. Then she hangs the sign on the headquarters wall. It says:

#DRESSCODED FOR HAVING HAIR.

Mom is getting nervous about Danny coming home. I can tell because she spent the whole day cleaning the house. She searched every inch of Danny's room before she cleaned it.

"Do you want to sit out on the deck with me and watch the lightning bugs?" she asks.

"Yes. But I still need to write down some notes for the board of education meeting."

"Do you want *me* there?"

I need to think about this one. It could look bad showing up with parents, or it could make it clear we have their support.

"Yes. That would be good."

Mom turns on the outside speakers and puts on her favorite band, the Indigo Girls. She pours us some seltzer and brings out a big bowl of buttery popcorn.

"So what's the Dan Plan?" I ask.

"Well, the school said he can still take final exams next week, so he's been studying. And then Daddy and I are thinking it's probably best if he spends the summer at Granny's."

"Wait, really?"

"Yes. Granny is actually good for him. We told her the truth, and she took it very well and reminded us of Aunt

Maggie's 'issues' when she was a teenager. So it's Danny and Granny's summer adventure."

"Wow. I want a summer adventure."

"We'll have one on our girls' trip." She takes a sip of seltzer. "It's good for Danny to get away from all the bad influences."

Mom doesn't quite get that *Danny* is the bad influence.

We're about to write our road-trip idea list when Thibodeaux starts barking like crazy at a figure standing to the side of our deck.

"Hello," Mom calls out, turning down the music.

"Hi, I'm looking for Molly Frost." It's a girl's voice.

"I'm Molly."

She walks toward us and stands at the steps. "Sorry. I tried the doorbell, but then I heard music back here. Uh, my mom is in the driveway. I just, I heard the podcasts, and I wanted to tell you my story."

I recognize her. She's the girl who left school last year. She's the one who got dress coded for being sick.

"Oh. Okay. Great." I motion for her to follow me.

Our moms talk on the deck while we take the lantern up to the tree house.

Her name is Catherine. She's in ninth grade. And she remembers that day like it was yesterday.

DRESS CODED: A PODCAST

ME: Hello, Fisher Middle School and beyond. My name is Molly Frost, and this is *Dress Coded: A Podcast*, episode nine. Please remember to show up at the board of education meeting this Friday, June 8, at seven o'clock. We are going to make our case at the end of the meeting, during the comments section. Tonight, we welcome a special guest. So, Catherine, do you want to tell us about yourself?

CATHERINE: I'm in ninth grade, and I left the district after a really upsetting dress-coding situation last year.

ME: What happened?

CATHERINE: It was a lot of things. Fingertip, or . . .

She whispers, "What's her name?" I shrug.

CATHERINE: Well, she targeted me from the first day of seventh grade. I'm kind of big-boned, and shorts don't fit me that great. There was only one pair that I really felt comfortable in, and I wore them all the time, even though I kept getting pulled over and sent down to the office. After my mom had to bring me new clothes a few times, she threw out my favorite shorts and grounded me for not following the school handbook.

ME: I'm really sorry.

CATHERINE: It's okay. She feels bad about it now. Then once, I was wearing leggings, and Dr. Couchman pulled me over in front of this kid I liked. He told me I was inviting boys to stare at me and it would be easier for everyone if I dressed more like a lady.

ME: What did you say?

CATHERINE: Nothing. I didn't want to get grounded again. So I dressed all frumpy the rest of the year, and everything was fine until I got sick. I had a high fever, and I felt like I was going to faint. I was trying to get to the nurse, and I was burning up, so I took off my sweater and leaned my head against the wall to cool off for a minute. That's when Fingertip started flipping out on me. I kept asking if I could go to the nurse, but she wouldn't let me.

ME: That's horrible.

CATHERINE: Yeah. After a while, Ms. Lane came out of her classroom and put her arm around me and took me to the nurse. I love Ms. Lane.

ME: Everybody loves Ms. Lane. So how did that make you feel?

CATHERINE: Honestly, I was so sick I just wanted to go home and sleep. But then my parents decided it was not a good school environment for me, and I transferred to Catholic.

ME: Is it better there?

CATHERINE: I'd rather wear a uniform than be followed around and yelled at.

"Can I say something else?" she whispers. I nod.

CATHERINE: If you're listening, Ms. Lane, I just want to say thank you.

ME: Do you think there should be any dress code at Fisher Middle?

She stares at me and taps her foot on the floor.

CATHERINE: No. Just leave people alone. Middle school is hard enough.

- Drama
- Bullies
- Braces
- Bad lunches
- Code Reds
- Code Yellows
- Code Browns
- Sunday nights
- Homework
- Tests
- Quizzes
- Climate change
- Parents taking phones away
- Losing Snapchat streaks
- Presentations (in front of everyone)
- Backstabbing
- Broken hearts
- Pimples
- Loneliness
- Stress
- Sports failures
- Embarrassing parents
- Embarrassing body parts

- Embarrassing everything
- Falling asleep before you finish studying
- Waking up late
- Nothing to wear
- Nothing to do
- Nothing to say
- Nothing but . . .
- Drama

IF YOU'RE GOING TO BE A TOAD,
YOU MIGHT AS WELL BE GOLDEN

Navya and I are in the library, writing out a two-minute speech for the board meeting tonight on why we think the dress code should be eliminated from the handbook. Everybody says they'll be there, except Ashley—that's no big surprise.

Mr. Beam, the librarian, drops a blue folder on the table, winks, adjusts his tie, and walks away. Navya and I look at each other. If Mr. Beam were an animal, he would be the grandchild of a butterfly, a porcupine, an ostrich, and one of those hot-dog dogs.

Navya opens the folder. It's stacked with articles about dress-code protests and how, by law, student dress codes cannot be unevenly enforced.

The bell rings, and we gather up the articles and stuff them back in the blue folder.

"Thank you, Mr. Beam," I call into his office, where he is chugging a Pepsi. He flaps his hand like a butterfly wing. We wave back.

o o o

Mary Kate practices her science presentation on the bus ride home.

"Golden toads have been extinct since 1989."

"Why?" I ask.

"Molly, let me actually give the presentation."

"Did you choose the golden toad in honor of your nickname?"

"I don't know. Come on, Molly. I hate giving presentations. Will you let me practice?"

She reads from the index cards without looking up. After three five-minute run-throughs, we reach our stop.

"Well?" she says.

"I miss the golden toads, and I never even knew them," I say.

"Me too."

"Tonight?"

"I'll be there."

We gather in front of the old Fisher Middle School, a brick building sticking out like a sore thumb between the tennis courts and the convenience store. These days, the old school is mostly used for meetings and equipment storage and the annual Halloween haunted house to benefit our athletic program.

Megan shows up wearing a T-shirt that says Stop Shaming Girls.

"Wow. Nice," I say, wishing I had coordinated a T-shirt brigade.

We sit in the front section of the old FMS auditorium, near the microphone, so we can be ready to make our public statements at the end of the meeting.

"Good thing we got here early," Navya's mom says.

The auditorium is packed with adults. My friends and I are the only ones here under the age of forty.

"We should have recruited more people," Liza says.

"I posted it on Instagram. I thought more people would be here," I say.

We've decided Navya and I will speak together, and everyone else will stand around us at the mic. My hands are sweating a little. It's a lot of pressure to say what we need to say in two minutes.

First up are announcements and other business. Then the fight starts over whether or not to convert the athletic fields from regular grass to artificial turf. It's literally a fight. Adults are yelling at each other. One guy stands up and sticks his finger in the chest of another guy. There's a lot of talking about the budget. A bunch of moms are saying the crumb rubber will cause cancer. And the finger-pointing guy is calling them nutjobs. Mom's leg starts shaking, which means she's about to blow.

Two hours. Our community fights over fields for two hours before the board chair asks Finger Pointer to leave and calls for an end to the discussion, because she wants to get to bear hunting.

"The bears are taking over the town," an elderly lady says. "Somebody is going to get hurt. It's time to do something drastic."

"What do you want to do? Start shooting them off your back porch?" a guy asks. "We live in the suburbs. It's ridiculous to say you're going to start hunting bears in the middle of this town. How about not leaving your garbage out? That's what's bringing them here."

Traps. People want to lay giant bear traps behind our school.

In *our* woods. So *we* can stumble upon baby bears screaming for their moms.

I want to stand up and say something so badly, but I have to wait for my issue.

After ninety minutes of bear debates, I look over at Pearl. She's fast asleep.

"We're going to direct this to the town council," the chair finally says.

"What?" Liza says out loud. "After all this?"

It's almost eleven, and people start getting up to leave.

I panic and jump up, motioning for Navya to come with me. I lean into the mic.

"Don't we get to make public comments about other business?" I ask loudly, my hands shaking by my side.

More people are talking in groups and making their way to the doors.

The board members stare down at us from the stage.

The chair says, "We've gone too long as it is. We'll table your comments for next time."

" 'Next time,' meaning September?"

"Yes." She looks down at her notes. "September fifteenth is our next meeting. Thank you, everyone."

"But nothing even got done here," I say. Laughter erupts around me.

The chair gets up and walks out through the back of the stage.

Then the woman with the bob haircut.

Then the two men with matching glasses.

Then the woman with the red pumps.

And the two women whispering.

And the man tossing all their water bottles into the recycling bin.

Just like that, the board of education has left the building.

"That's it?" Mary Kate asks. "I can't believe this."

We're all stunned. We just sat through this miserable

and boring display of adult embarrassment, and we don't even get two minutes.

"Listen, girls. By September you'll be ready to make a splash," Navya's mom says.

"We're ready to make a splash now, Mom," Navya says, "and that's a weird saying."

Mary Kate and Lucy follow the crowd up the auditorium aisle.

I stick my note cards in my pocket and take a slightly melted Christmas Hershey's Kiss from Megan.

"Well, that's a wrap," Bea says. "We tried, guys."

We file out one by one, dejected and annoyed. And then I glance back and see Olivia still sitting in her seat, her hands folded in her lap, staring straight ahead.

"Do you want a ride, Olivia?" I ask.

"Nope," she says. "I'm not leaving."

DRESS CODED: A PODCAST

ME: Hello, Fisher Middle School and beyond. My name is Molly Frost, and this is *Dress Coded: A Podcast*. Tonight, I come to you live from the old middle school, where we have decided to stage a sit-in to protest the unfair dress code at Fisher Middle. Olivia, can you tell our audience what we're hoping to accomplish?

OLIVIA: We are hoping to get rid of the dress code in the Fisher Middle School handbook. They never enforce the dress code at the high school, and the students seem to be educated just fine when they graduate.

ME: And, Navya, can you explain why we felt like we needed to do this?

NAVYA: We sent a petition to the interim superintendent a few weeks ago. We still haven't gotten a response. We just sat for hours trying to bring the dress code to the attention of the board of education, and they wouldn't even give us two minutes to talk about it. But they had time to talk about crumb-rubber turf fields and how to murder bears. I play sports, and the field thing is an important topic, but so is making girls feel bad literally every single day of middle school.

ME: Liza, do you want to add anything?

LIZA: We're not going to stop until you change the handbook. We're not scared little kids anymore.

THE OPPOSITE OF A CAMPOUT

Mr. Ricky, the custodian, speed-walks down to the stage, where we're all sitting with our legs dangling.

"What's going on here?" he asks Liza's mom.

"The students are protesting the school dress code," she says calmly.

"Well, nobody told me anything about this. I gotta clear out the auditorium and clean up."

Mr. Ricky sweeps the stage and walks up and down the aisles, checking for trash.

We sit, Olivia and Pearl, Liza and Navya, Bea, Megan, my mom, Liza's and Navya's moms, and me.

"What are we doing?" Liza asks.

"I'm staying," Olivia says. "We did everything we were supposed to do, and nothing worked. I'm staying until they listen to us."

"Time to clear out," Mr. Ricky says, looking a little nervous. "Gotta lock up now."

We all look at each other.

"It's not Mr. Ricky's problem," Liza says.

Pearl stands up. "I have an idea. We need our tents."

"Okay, I'm listening," Olivia says.

"We skip the camping trip and set up our tents out near the garden."

"Yes. I love it. We have a camp-in. Like a sit-in, but in tents," Bea says.

Pearl smiles. "Precisely."

Mom tries to exhaust us with her questions about whether or not this is legal and what our rights are on school property.

"Mom, it's called peaceful resistance. We'll take our chances," I say, patting Pearl on the back.

"So it's a plan?" Pearl asks, looking at Olivia.

"It's a plan," Olivia says.

o o o

Navya, Bea, and Pearl go with Navya's mom to pick up all the camping gear.

We debate whether or not to write something to everyone in our class. They ask me to do it, Queen of the Podcast, Princess of Detention.

I write this in the 217-person group chat:

Dear Classmates,

As you know, many of us are sick of the way administrators and some teachers enforce the dress code at Fisher Middle School. We sent a petition to the interim superintendent. We have complained, protested with signs, and shared stories with our Dress Coded podcast. But nothing has changed. Girls before us tried to take this issue to the board of education, and we did too. But nothing changed.

243

So we have decided to stage a CAMP-IN. We will no longer be going to Strawberry Hill. We are very sorry to the parents who worked hard to make this trip happen and the parents who gave $25. But we want to show our school district that we care about the girls who will be at Fisher Middle next year and all the years after. We want the dress code removed from the Fisher handbook. There is no dress code at the high school, or if there is, nobody enforces it, and they have survived. Why is there one at the middle school? We are 12, 13, and 14 years old! If you want to join us, please meet at the Kindness Garden with your camping stuff as soon as you can get here. Bring signs if you want. We could get in trouble (just so you know), but we are ready for that.

Sincerely,
The White Dresses

I don't want to see the comments. I don't need to see Nick and company ripping into us. "Let's leave the group," I suggest to my friends. We all leave except Liza. She wants to see what people are saying.

How does my heart know that my finger just deleted a group chat? How does it know to beat faster? How does my heart know I'm suddenly terrified?

By midnight, it looks like we've convinced over forty people to come to our camp-in. By 12:15, it's sixty-two.

Under the light of the moon, the blinding lights over the tennis courts, and our phone flashlights, we drag all our camping stuff to the clearing between the garden and the woods.

Mom deserves the Mom of the Year Award for sleeping in our minivan next to the circle of tents.

I snuggle in between Bea and Megan, and we are asleep before we can say *Are we really doing this?*

THE TENT VILLAGERS

We need to be prepared for Dr. Couchman. It's only a matter of time before he shows up. Everyone knows he never misses an episode of *Dress Coded: A Podcast*.

Liza's mom arrives with orange juice and donuts.

"Come eat," Mom says.

"In a minute." I'm dragging a tag-sale sandwich board across the lawn. END THE UNFAIR DRESS CODE, it says in giant red letters on both sides. It's a beautiful day, cloudless and warm, but not too hot.

My neck hurts and my hair is greasy, but I'm no longer nervous about this decision. Now I'm just ready to be seen.

People start rolling in. They unload their camping stuff at the curb. And then more people arrive: girls from my class, girls from Mary Kate's class, girls who were dress coded nearly every day, and girls who were never dress coded.

The targets.

The invisibles.

The in-betweens.

I walk over to Mary Kate. "I can't believe your mom let you come."

"She called your mom at seven in the morning, and they talked for a long time. At first, she thought I was being disrespectful, and she was worried Couchman would take all this out on me next year, but whatever your mom said worked."

I look over at Mom, who has spent a lot more than twenty-five dollars on food for this, even though our family is struggling more now that they have to pay for Danny's appointments.

I run over and give her a hug. "Thank you for this, Mom."

"I'm so proud of you," she says, squeezing my arm.

We get busy putting up tents and setting up our sandwich board in the center of the Kindness Garden, next to the bird-bath. People add signs to the board, and Megan's mom drops off a big box of white T-shirts and fabric markers.

"Good idea," Bea says, scooping up a T-shirt and spreading out a picnic blanket on the grass next to the lilac tree.

At 11:45, Tom gets out of his dad's truck with a sleeping bag and a lunch box. "Tom, what you are doing here?" I ask, running over to him.

"Will told me the camping trip is here now."

"But did he tell you we're doing a protest against the dress code, and we might get in trouble?"

"Yeah, I know. That's okay. I told my parents I want to support you."

"Aww. Thanks, Tom."

A few minutes later, Will and Clay and Chen come wandering out of the woods. They're carrying a tent and backpacks and s'mores sticks, and Clay is wheeling Will's portable fire pit. I don't know why, but seeing them smiling their goofy smiles almost gets me choked up.

There used to be dozens of eighth-grade groups, each

of them clustered together like schools of fish, zigzagging through the hallways, always changing formation. Now, there are two: the group that is going to Strawberry Hill State Park and the group that is protesting the Fisher Middle School dress code. I've never been more sure of which group I want to swim with.

I guess Ashley must feel the same.

> **ME:** Ashley, don't you care about this at all?

> **ASHLEY:** It's just not that big of a deal. Why can't you guys stop harassing me about this?

I'm not mad.
I'm also not surprised.
Olivia texts, **CODE JIM**, and everyone gathers around the sandwich board carrying signs and wearing slogans on white T-shirts.
The parents stay back near the tents.
This is our fight.

THE LETTER IN MY HEAD

Dear Dr. Couchman,

What if on the first day of school you welcomed seventh graders with words of encouragement and praise? What if you told them Fisher Middle School would be a safe, warm place where they could learn, discover their passions, and find ways to lift one another up? What if instead of wasting a whole assembly on dress codes, you spent that time teaching us how to treat peers with dignity and respect, how to cheer each other on and comfort each other when we're struggling?

Because we will struggle. At home. At school. Inside our own heads and bodies.

What if you carried a laminated paper that said "Wear what's comfortable. Wear what makes you feel confident and strong. Look at the student next to you and behind you and in front of you and acknowledge that they are wearing what makes them feel confident and strong. And it's all good."

What if, instead of seeing us as covered or uncovered body parts, you saw us as people and you learned *our names? And our talents? And pushed us to be who we were meant to be?*

It's not about the clothes, Dr. Couchman. It never has been.

Sincerely,
Molly

COUCHMAN UNCOVERS OUR
BIRTHDAY-SUIT GRAND PLAN

His face is the color of a sliced tomato. He's wearing golf clothes and sandals, and his arms are moving wildly as he marches toward us.

"What is going on here?"

Olivia looks at me. I look at Pearl. Pearl looks at me. I step forward. I'm not scared of him. Not at all.

"We are here to protest the Fisher Middle School dress code. We would like you to remove the dress code from the handbook," I say calmly. "Previous efforts have gone nowhere, and we are here to show you how serious this is to us."

He grins, which makes me furious.

"Okay, this is absurd. How about we just let you come to school in your birthday suits. Will that make you happy? Come on, pack it up. You're on school property, and you need to leave."

We don't move.

"We're not leaving," Olivia says, looking him squarely in the eyes. "We're not leaving until you take our request seriously. And just so you know, the TV news will be here soon."

Olivia is bluffing. But that's actually a great idea. Bad guys hate the press.

"Welp, I'm going to need to call the board of ed to see how we can get you off our property. And they're not going to like being bothered on a Saturday."

"Leave us alone," Liza shouts.

"Leave us alone," we chant, over and over again.

He storms away, tripping over a pile of kindness rocks, which he kicks with his sandal. We don't stop chanting until he and his stubbed toe are gone.

THE CAMP-IN IS MORE FUN THAN
WE THOUGHT IT WOULD BE

We play horseshoes.

We eat the food our parents bring us.

We choreograph a dance.

We hunt for rocks and paint newer, better kindness slogans.

We toast marshmallows in the portable fire pit.

We make space for Ms. Lane and Ms. Santos-Skinner, who show up in sneakers and sweatpants with a two-woman tent and a giant basket of homemade blueberry muffins.

We sit on blankets, and two girls who were both in a lot of my classes this year set up a karaoke machine. Tom goes first. He sings "Hallelujah," and people cry. Talia says he has perfect pitch. She asks Tom to sing a duet, and they're so good they could do this for a living.

"They're like garden angels," Mom says, with her eyes bugging out of her head.

Everybody wants to sing, so Megan holds on to a sign-up clipboard and calls out names. Clay and Will sing a K-pop song (because Will found out Pearl likes K-pop, but he doesn't know Pearl likes K-pop because she found out Bea likes K-pop).

∘ ∘ ∘

Right after we all sing the *Hamilton* soundtrack and just as Navya's mom shows up with giant bags of kettle corn, four cars roll into the parking lot.

The doors open and Dr. Couchman, Mr. Dern, Fingertip, and all the members of the board of education step out. One guy is dressed in a tuxedo. Either he's really mad that we pulled him away from something fancy, or really glad we got him out of a boring event.

Megan turns off the music, and we all stand up and walk toward the side of the school building.

"Who's in charge of this thing?" Dr. Couchman asks.

Tiny camera lights flash on all around me. They make me braver, because I know so many more people will see this.

"We all are," I say. "We are all sick of the way you bully us over the dress code."

"Hi, everybody. I'm Mae Dunn, chair of the board." She steps forward and looks around. "So I'm hearing you're all here to protest the dress code, right?"

Olivia steps forward. "We feel the dress code unfairly targets girls and is not evenly enforced. We are asking that you remove the dress code and allow children to wear what makes them comfortable."

Everyone cheers.

Olivia's stepdad is a lawyer. He told her to make sure she mentions the evenly enforced part, because it's against the Constitution for schools to dress code one girl but not another if they're wearing the exact same thing.

Mae Dunn smiles. "Well, first of all, we appreciate all of

you taking the time to show up for this protest. I see you are very passionate. I am almost positive the board reviewed this some time ago." She looks at the elderly man next to her. "Burt, where did we end up on that?"

Burt shrugs. "Not sure. Would have to look into it."

"You ended up nowhere," I say, "according to our high school sources. And we tried to get this on your June agenda, but you said you had to focus on crumb-rubber playing fields and bear killing. And we sent a petition to the interim superintendent almost a month ago, and we haven't heard anything. Not a word."

Mae Dunn smiles again. "Well, how about this? I can call a closed board meeting for early next week to review dress code policy. Does anyone know if they enforce the dress code at the high school?"

"No, they don't," we all say at the same time.

"Okay, so we will call the meeting, but we need you to pack it up and head home. This is school property, and we can't have you sleeping here."

We freeze.

We need to make a quick decision. We can't look like we're not organized.

"We're going to stay," I say.

Fingertip and Dr. Couchman look like they're about to hyperventilate.

"I can't allow that," Dr. Couchman says. "Let's go. Everybody out of here."

The parents are standing in a group on the edge of the parking lot.

"Nope. Not going," Liza says. Everyone's phone goes up.

"Okay, then. For the record, let it be known you are staying on school property at your own risk. And the fire marshal is going to want you to put out that fire. Will you do that for us?" Mae Dunn points at the portable fire pit.

"That's it? You're letting them stay?" Dr. Couchman says, throwing up his arms.

"How do you presume we drag all these people out?" Mae Dunn asks.

"Thank you," I say. "We'll be waiting for your decision."

And that's how we leave it.

We sing. We dance. We eat popcorn by lantern light. We tell ghost stories in groups of eight, ten, twelve. We hear our parents laughing in chairs by the birdbath. We look up at the stars and guess each other's futures.

We sleep well, even with the bears and the ticks and the abnormally chilly night air and the looming threat of a big fat *we're too busy, so we'll just wait for these kids to get sick of camping and go home* from the board of education.

At one in the morning, my phone rings. I wake up totally confused.

It's Jessica. "Molly, we're here."

"Where?"

"Outside. Can we sleep in your tent?"

Megan is squished up against the side of the tent, and Olivia and Pearl are next to her.

"Who's we?"

"Jasmine and me. Where are you?"

I walk out of the tent and shine my phone flashlight around. Jasmine and Jessica are standing near the side doorway of the school in their prom dresses, holding sleeping bags.

"You came from prom? You look so pretty."

"We left our dates at the after-party," Jessica says. "We really wanted to be here."

They follow me to our tent.

"How was it?" I ask.

"Really fun," Jasmine says. "But it's over. And we're ready to protest."

We whisper until the first light of morning streams through the tent flaps.

When this all started, I never, ever imagined I would be sleeping in a tent with seniors on their prom night.

Dress Coded: A Podcast has changed everything.

It's weird to see people from my school with matted-down hair roaming around the campsite in pajamas.

We call a meeting at nine o'clock. Jessica and Jasmine are sitting on the bench, wrapped in their sleeping bags, giving seventh graders dating advice.

"How about Rahul? He'd be a great prom date," Mom says. Mom doesn't even need to see people in prom dresses to trigger her prom obsessive disorder.

Megan's dad brings bagels, and everyone sits on the tennis court, because the grass is still damp with dew.

Olivia and I take turns talking. People nod and clap, and we all decide we're going to stay until the handbook changes or the cops drag us out. We arrange to go home in shifts, so most of us are always here.

I really, really hope I'm not still sleeping in a tent at Fisher Middle when high school starts.

We take the trash home with us, shower, and come back to the tent village so the next group can go. We don't have money to buy big group meals, so people eat at home and bring snacks with them. By the time we've all gone home and come back, it's late afternoon and we're ready for more karaoke.

We lose a bunch of seventh graders because their parents don't want them to have targets on their backs next year. We totally get it. But we gain a bunch of girls from Strawberry Hill who, after they got there and had to deal with Nick and his friends making fun of us and them and each other, really regretted not being with us.

"What did we miss?" Navya asks a group of girls from the lacrosse team who are having a hard time putting up their tent.

They list a bunch of things:

- Nick got in trouble for pranking people by throwing eggs in their tents.
- The baseball players played catch literally the whole time.
- Chris Reynolds cried because he stepped on glass, and somebody's mom had to pull it out of his foot.
- Jack Reese ate a mushroom on a dare, and Brad's mom panicked and brought him to the hospital in case it was poisonous.
- The water was too cold for swimming.
- Ashley didn't say much or do much.

"Sounds great," Navya says sarcastically. "Really sad I missed it."

Pearl drags Navya and me into the tent and asks us to ask Bea if she might possibly, slightly have feelings for Pearl. We corner Bea on the way to my house to use our bathroom.

She seems surprised and then says Pearl is amazing but she doesn't like her that way. She says she doesn't like anyone that way right now.

We're stuck in a dysfunctional love triangle.

We don't want to crush Will or Pearl, or make things weird with any of them, so we decide to be terrible people and avoid them all.

Liza and I sit on the bench near the lilac tree sipping lemonade through stainless-steel straws and watching our classmates sing old Taylor Swift songs.

"Remember when our moms wouldn't let us go to the Taylor Swift concert because they didn't want to get stuck in concert traffic?" I say.

"Yes. We were so irritated we hid under my bed for hours."

"It was probably five minutes."

"Time is weird when you're little." Liza flicks a slow-moving beetle off her grass-stained knee. She pauses. "Moll, have you noticed most of our conversations have to do with reminiscing about the past? Like, whenever we talk, we're always remembering the good times we had."

I try to read the expression on her face. "Yeah, that's true, but it's because we had so many good times. That was the best summer of my life."

"I know. Me too. But sometimes I wish we were making new memories instead of always remembering the old ones."

My stomach aches a little, and I know what she means. I honestly don't know if we miss each other or if we miss the summer before seventh grade, or both.

"Today is a new one," I say. "We won't forget this, that's for sure."

"No, we won't forget this."

I pull a lilac off a low branch and tuck it behind Liza's ear. *"Bonita,"* I say. Before we get up, I kiss her on the cheek. "We're going to make memories this summer so when high school is over we can meet back on this bench and remember it all, okay?"

Liza smiles. "It's a date."

The whole day, Dr. Couchman's red car and Mr. Dern's black Jeep drive back and forth on the main road. They move so slowly the people behind them honk.

Somebody decides to run up to the sidewalk with a **LEAVE US ALONE** sign. Others follow.

Couchman and Dern don't come back.

IF YOU EVER PLAY TRUTH OR DARE, TAKE THE DARE. TRUST ME.

I know it's a bad idea, but I agree to do it anyway.

Will wants to play truth or dare, and he convinces Rahul, Chen, Clay, and Tom to get a bunch of people together in front of his tent.

After a few warm-up questions that result in Liza eating a miniature pine cone and Chen admitting he's scared of cats, the obviously planned question pops up.

Rahul asks Pearl if she likes anyone.

Pearl says, "Next question."

Rahul glances over at Will, who is looking down at his phone. "Do you have feelings for anyone?" Rahul says.

Pearl throws a pine cone at the tent. It bounces off the side flap and hits Clay in the head. "Okay, this is stupid. Will, I like you as a friend. I think you're the nicest kid in our class. But I don't *like* like you. I'm really sorry."

Will gets up and brushes off his pants. "I'm out."

He walks toward the woods. I follow him and grab his sweatshirt.

"Can you stop for a minute?"

He turns. "You knew, didn't you?"

I nod. "I didn't want to hurt you."

"Oh, so you let me be humiliated in front of everyone?"

"I'm really, really sorry. I guess I should just tell you that

Pearl likes Bea. And Bea doesn't like Pearl. So it's just one big sad Shakespeare play."

"She likes Bea?"

"Yeah. She's out to her family and friends, but it's not like she's broadcasting it on a global level."

He sits on the ground and shakes his head. "Have you ever felt pain in your heart? Like an ache?"

"Yeah, Will. I feel it all the time."

"This is awful."

"I know."

"I'm going to go home now. I just need to be alone."

EVEN FROGS HAVE A BREAKING POINT

Mom calls me home for dinner. I rush back and search the pantry for toppings for our ice cream sundae bar, an annual almost-summer tradition that started a long time ago.

Mom made fish-and-chips and broccoli, and decorated the table out on the deck with flowers and candles.

Dad comes in from the garage, holding a squirming Thibodeaux like a baby. "Hey, Molls. Boy, your mom says you've become quite the activist. I'm proud of you."

"Really?"

"Heck yeah. The only thing I ever organized was a battle of the bands."

"That's actually pretty cool, Dad. Hey, can you make me a protest playlist?"

"Oooh. That I can do."

Mom calls up to Danny, who had slipped in through the front door. "Come on down, Dan."

After fifteen minutes of trying to get Danny downstairs, Mom gives up. Normally, she would look sad and bring a tray to his room and sulk around. But tonight, she sits down and spreads her napkin on her lap and says, "Dig in."

Dad wants to know all about the camp-in. I tell him to

come over with me after dinner, and he can find out for himself.

Danny comes just as Mom is setting up the sundae bar.

"You know what, Dan? Your mom made your favorite dinner, and you couldn't even bother to come down." Dad's irritated.

"I was unpacking."

"Not an excuse," Mom says.

The fireflies scatter. I don't think they like it when Danny's home.

"Are you even going to say hi to Molly?" Mom asks, shaking her head.

"Hi, Frog. You're looking unattractive today."

I ignore him and look at Mom. "Can I eat my sundae now? I have to go get ready."

"Ready for what?" Danny is suddenly curious about my life.

I stop and look at him. "I'm going to a protest I organized. You can make fun of me if you want, but I should warn you it's not going to make me feel bad or question myself. And you can call me Frog, but I don't care. I like frogs. Good luck studying. I hope you do really well on your exams."

Danny grabs a pint of ice cream and goes back upstairs. Dad, Mom, and I make one giant sundae with mountains of whipped cream and all the toppings.

"More for the rest of us," Dad says, wiping purple sprinkles off his beard.

I run upstairs to dress in layers, grab a few extra blankets, brush my teeth, and call out to Dad to drive me back to the middle school. When we get there, somebody has put cones in front of the entrance so cars can't drive up. Dad parks at the store across the street and walks me to our tent village.

"Promise you won't sign up for karaoke, no matter how much you want to," I say.

"Oh, Moll. I don't think I can promise that."

THE LETTER I SLIDE UNDER
MY BROTHER'S DOOR

Dear Danny,

Once upon a time, I loved you so much I didn't even care if you called me ugly or pushed me down and split open my lip or stole all my Halloween candy and blamed it on goblins. I loved you, and I would have done anything to get you to love me back.

I cleaned your room for you and went to the store for you and went downstairs just to get you snacks and soda and gave you my birthday money. I even lied for you and hid your nasty nicotine and pretended it was all okay because it gave you a reason to go into my room and talk to me and make me feel like a sister.

For a long, long time I held on to our trip to Atlantis, not only because it was the best day of my life, but because I believed every day could be like that if I just tried harder.

But I'm done trying, Danny. I'm a good sister. I always have been. You're just a bad brother.

I still love you so much. But I'm not going to give you my energy. I'm going to keep it for all the

important things I want to do. I wish you well,
my brother.

Molly

I read it to Megan under the phone flashlight. The tears wet
my pillow. She listens and nods.

"Good?" I ask.

"Perfect," she says.

We're lying in the tent, talking, when Navya sticks her head in.

"Molly, Ms. Lane is asking for you."

"Ms. Lane?"

"Yes, Ms. Lane. Come on."

I feel around for my flip-flops and smooth down my ponytail before following Navya down to the tennis court. Ms. Lane is standing next to her car with her favorite person.

"Hi, Ms. Lane."

"Molly, you remember Ms. Milholland?"

"Yes, hi." I'm a little confused.

We sit on the bench, and Ms. Milholland turns her body to fully face me. "I've been following you girls and your podcasts, and Ms. Lane has been filling me in."

"Really?"

"Oh, for sure. I've stayed out of it, but I know a lot of your teachers aren't happy about all the dress coding and body shaming that's happening. I don't want to step on any toes, but I get an earful at our monthly potlucks."

I have a feeling Dr. Couchman, Mr. Dern, and Fingertip aren't invited to these monthly potlucks.

"Listen, I had an idea," she says, taking my hand with

her thin, bony fingers. "What if I can get you all a proper emergency board meeting tomorrow night? One open to the public so you all can make your case. And in return, you kids pack it up and stop giving Dr. Couchman a coronary?"

I hesitate. "The board chair said she would have a meeting, but we have a feeling they'll just make excuses to ignore us. And, Ms. Milholland, we really don't want the sixth graders to have to deal with this. It's important to us."

She nods. "I understand. And I applaud you all for your act of resistance. How about I negotiate a real meeting with a guaranteed decision? I've still got some pull on that board. In fact, Mae owes me one for sewing her pants when she split them right up the tush in third grade."

We laugh.

"I have to talk to my friends," I say.

"You do that, honey."

○ ○ ○

It's late.

We don't have the time or energy to call everybody to the tennis court, so we do what all red-blooded American teenagers do when they need to make a decision.

We send out a group text.

We weigh the pros and cons of packing up, going home, and taking our concerns to another board of education meeting.

Pros of going with the Milholland Plan:

- We have Ms. Milholland behind us, and everyone loves her.
- If the board of education votes to keep the dress code, we can come back out here.
- We will have a chance to tell our stories and give good arguments.
- We can go home, shower, and sleep in our own beds.

Cons of going with the Milholland Plan:

- We said we weren't leaving until they had a decision, and that might make us look weak.
- It's fun making Dr. Couchman and Fingertip squirm.

We end up going with the Milholland Plan. I call Ms. Lane, and, within an hour, this letter goes out to all the FMS parents:

Dear Parents and Guardians,

As you probably know, some of our FMS students have been staging a "camp-in" to protest what they feel is unfair dress-code enforcement. Our board understands their concerns, and we applaud their passionate use of peaceful demonstration as a tool to make their voices heard. The students have agreed to return home tonight, and we will meet tomorrow at 7:00 p.m. for

an emergency public board meeting to discuss the issue
of the dress code at the middle school. If you or your
child would like to speak, please limit your comments
to two minutes. We look forward to resolving this issue
quickly.

> *Best Wishes,*
> *Mae Dunn, MPH, MD*
> *Chair, Board of Education*

"I hope it's not just us and our moms," Olivia says as she helps Pearl take down our tent.

"It won't be." I look around at the people packing up. "There must be over two hundred people here. They're all in now."

BAD GHOSTS

In fourth grade, Will and I decorated the tree house with fake spiderwebs and plastic skeletons for Halloween. We went up at night with LED candles and a device Will swore was a ghost detector. He confessed he was born a ghost hunter and that he had never told anyone but he could see spirits and demons all over the place.

I could barely move, I was so afraid.

"Are there any here now?" I asked.

He made a creepy face and held the LED candle up to his eyes. "Unfortunately, yes. And they're very, very evil."

I started shaking, and Will grabbed the candles and took off, leaving me there to scream as loud as I could until Mrs. Brown up the street heard me and called my parents, who were watching a movie with the volume turned way up.

I slept between my parents in their bed for far too long, and eventually Will's mom made him admit he was making it all up. Even then, I didn't believe him.

o o o

I knock on Will's back door before school. He's in the kitchen eating cereal.

"Hi, Molly," his mom says, sliding open the screen. "Come in. How is our neighborhood revolutionary?"

"Fine, I guess."

Will doesn't look up.

"Will, come on, walk with Molly so I don't have to drive you."

"No, Mom. I'm tired. I need a ride."

She grabs him by the shoulders and pushes him out the door. We stand face-to-face, and I realize Will is suddenly a lot taller than me.

"I'm sorry," I say as he starts to walk away.

"You humiliated me."

"I didn't want to hurt your feelings, so I was just hoping it would go away."

"You knew how I felt about her. And you thought it would just go away?"

"Will, stop," I shout.

He stops.

"I'm sorry. I'm really, really sorry. And I know you're upset, but Pearl still wants to be your friend. And if it makes you feel better, we can be even for Ghost Hunter."

His face changes a little.

"You've been holding that over my head for years. Does this mean you're not going to bring that up again? If I forgive you?"

I hesitate. "Well, Ghost Hunter was way worse. Let's admit that."

"I don't think it was."

"Okay, it was. I slept in my parents' bed for months."

"Fine. I'll forgive you. But we have to be even. You

never get to mention Ghost Hunter again for the rest of our lives."

"Not even as a story to tell our kids someday?"

He stares at me. "I'm not having kids with you."

I laugh. "No, you freak. I mean not even as a story to tell your kids and my kids when they're visiting our parents for Christmas?"

"Is this really the kind of stuff girls think about?"

"So . . . even?"

"Even." He slaps me on the back and takes off running.

"Can you slow down?" I say.

"Shh." He stops and nods up at the tree ahead on our left.

A baby bear is hanging off a branch. I quickly scan the woods for the mom, but I don't see her.

"What do we do?" I whisper. "It's going to fall."

"Just go."

We walk slowly down the path, looking back every few seconds.

We hear a thump, and the cub lands squarely on the ground.

"Phew," I say. "That was close."

The bell rings.

We're late for the second to last day of school.

o o o

The teachers are as done as we are, which is why we watch movies in nearly every single class. They should just send us to the auditorium and show us all the same movie so I won't confuse *The Outsiders* with *A Journey Through Physics*.

"Two minutes to say what we need to say tonight isn't much time," I whisper to Megan. Mr. Lu is trying to figure out why the movie stopped.

"It must be the ghosts again," he says, squinting at his laptop.

Everybody is laughing because we can see all his private messages on the screen and he doesn't know it.

"You'll squeeze it all in," Megan says. "Just talk fast."

I read the dress code over and over to myself.

Each time, I'm a little more mad and a lot more determined.

Tom is more quiet than usual at lunch.

"Thanks for going to the camp-in. Did you have fun singing karaoke?" Navya asks, offering him a pretzel rod.

He nods.

"You okay, Tom?" Bea asks.

He nods.

"Come on, Tom. You can tell us," I say.

He slowly chews his sandwich. "I don't know where I'm going to sit for lunch next year. Whatever. It's okay."

Bea looks at me. "Oh, Tom. We'll be there. Even if we don't all have the same lunch period as you, at least one of us will. We're lunch-table friends until the last day of senior year."

He nods. "That's cool."

I know Tom can count on us, but after Ashley dropped us, I wonder if we can count on each other.

"Why aren't you eating, Molly?" Bea asks.

"Really bad nerves."

Fingertip comes in and paces around the front of the cafeteria. She twists her face like she just swallowed some liquid medicine and walks back out. I'm sure she's wondering what will happen to her job if we manage to get rid of the dress code.

I think we all have really bad nerves today.

LIP BALM ON FRIENDSHIP

Bea, Navya, and I knock on Ashley's front door. Her mom answers and lets us in. I hope Ashley's mom never has to play poker, because her face definitely gives away what she's thinking.

Ashley is sitting by the pool, scrolling through Instagram.

We run up behind her, and she looks surprised and sad, all at the same time.

"We still love you, you know," Navya says.

"I love you too."

It's like lip balm on chapped lips. It feels good for a few minutes, but the chapped lips are still there. I don't know if I'll still be friends with Ashley in high school, but right now, we all need lip balm.

We start to tell her what we're planning to say at the board of education meeting.

"Why do you have to be this way? Why can't you just be normal?" Ashley asks.

The lip balm is already wearing off.

Meanwhile, I get a flurry of messages from Pearl.

PEARL: I don't want to go tonight.

ME: What? Why???

PEARL: Navya told me what Bea said. I don't want to see her. It's literally the most embarrassing situation ever.

> **ME:** I'm really sorry, but please don't miss tonight. It's probably going to be like all the other awkward things in our lives. As my granny says, "Here today, gone tomorrow."

PEARL: Okay, that's not helpful. Help me. What do I do?

> **ME:** Bea will be normal if you are, just like you and Will.

PEARL: Should I talk to her?

> **ME:** She's right here. Do you want to FaceTime her?

PEARL: Uhhhhhhh. NO. Why didn't you tell me she was right there?

> **ME:** I don't know.

PEARL: Jeez, Molly.

DRESS CODED: A PODCAST

ME: Hello, Fisher Middle School and beyond. My name is Molly Frost, and this is *Dress Coded: A Podcast*, episode eleven. Tonight, we're broadcasting live at the old Fisher Middle School auditorium, where we are asking the board of education to end the dress code at Fisher Middle School and remove it from the handbook completely.

The auditorium is filling up. A lot of Fisher students are coming in now, and the board of education should be out soon.

ME: Dr. Couchman, Mr. Dern, the lady we call Fingertip *[my friends stifle laughter]*, and the other dress coders have made our school very stressful. I don't think they understand how hard it is to find something to wear in the morning that doesn't make you self-conscious. They make it so much worse. We just want to be kids a little while longer.

The board of education comes out from behind the stage and takes their seats. The room is noisy. Mae Dunn turns on her mic. I keep recording.

"Thank you all for coming on such short notice, and thank you to my colleagues who had to rearrange plans to make it here tonight." She looks down at a pile of papers. "So we are here to listen to the comments of students from Fisher Middle School as they appeal to our board to terminate the dress code."

I reach into the pocket of my shorts and pull out the kindness rock Violeta's mom gave me. *YOU'VE GOT THIS.* I hold it in my left hand and look down at the page I pulled from the handbook.

We hear chanting coming from outside. It gets louder and louder. The back doors push open, and Jessica and Jasmine come in with Olivia's sister, followed by dozens and dozens of high school students shouting "Enough is enough."

"Enough is enough."

"Enough is enough."

We look around, shocked by what we're seeing. They file down the rows and stand behind us—girls, boys, what seems to be most of our school and an endless stream of high schoolers, all continuing to shout "Enough is enough" as they find seats. Within a few minutes, they start to line the walls around the auditorium.

Liza is next to me. Her eyes are wide. *Wow,* she mouths. I shrug. I had no idea this many people would show up. Up in the corner, I see the Channel 2 newswoman, the one with the very white teeth and the very pregnant belly. Her baby must be jumping around in there with all this noise.

Mae Dunn stands up and raises her hands. It takes a while, but eventually everyone settles down.

"I can see we have a lot of emotion in the room. Let's keep this orderly so we can hear everyone. We have two mics in front of each aisle. If you'd like to speak, please line up behind the mics."

I freeze. When it was just seventh and eighth graders, I had planned to jump up and go to the front of the line. But now I'm terrified, and all the high school and adult eyes are on me to get things started.

I lean toward the mic, clear my throat, and start to read the Fisher Middle School dress code, an unlaminated version of Dr. Couchman's darling:

"The neckline of a shirt, top, or dress must touch the upper chest. No exposed cleavage will be permitted. The back of the shirt must cover the lower back when student is seated. No exposed midriffs will be permitted. No T-back tank tops, camisoles, or shirts with large armholes will be permitted. T-shirts extending below the fingertips must be tucked in."

A guy yells "Fingertip" from the back of the room, and everybody laughs. I wait a few seconds and start again.

"No overly tight or revealing garments. Hemlines of shorts, skirts, and dresses will reach below the student's extended fingertips while standing. Inseams must be five inches or longer. No unusual hair colors, styles."

I read every last word of the Fisher Middle School dress code.

The buzzer sounds. My two minutes is up.

Then one by one, they come up, speak up, make their stories known.

The stories are all different, but the same.

One girl hid in the bathroom because she was so afraid of Dr. Couchman.

A trans girl was taunted by Mr. Dern for wearing lipstick.

The same girl was told she has to wear pants and a shirt and tie or miss Moving Up Day, even though her mom bought her a beautiful white dress.

Another girl wore sweatpants with words on the butt and was forced to wear that horrible animal-hair-, cigarette-, and rotten-banana-smelling burgundy sweater all day.

The Shame Sweater.

Liza tells the story of her very first mortifying day at Fisher Middle School.

A junior named Gabriel climbs up and freezes for a minute. It's obvious he's really nervous.

"It's okay," Mae Dunn says. "Take your time." He tells us about his sister, who is now at a boarding school in Massachusetts. She was so self-conscious, so afraid of getting pulled over all the time because she couldn't find clothes that fit, that she ended up refusing to go to school. She had to go to therapy and be tutored at home because she was so traumatized. "Fisher Middle School took away my sister's dignity. This has to stop."

Gabriel turns up the aisle, and Jessica goes next.

I watch Gabriel walk over to his friends. He's cute. And kind. And very cute.

High school is suddenly looking even more promising.

Talia tells her story, and the room goes silent.

Teachers are lined up against the wall, listening with horrified expressions. Parents give each other looks and shake their heads. As Talia turns away from the mic, Ms. Milholland reaches out and squeezes her arm.

A junior boy comes up and tells us that he is distracted by girls all day every day (everyone laughs), but it has nothing to do with the thickness of their shoulder straps or whether their shorts are longer than their fingertips. "That, my friends, is preposterous."

Every so often, "Enough is enough" erupts again.

A man goes up to the mic and clears his throat. "I just want to say these kids all need a good kick in the pants for what they're pulling here." People boo.

"Let him have his time," Mae Dunn says.

"You're being disrespectful. It's disgusting that you kids can't even wear decent clothes without protesting. You're spoiled rotten, and I hope this board puts you in your place."

A lot of boos and some claps fill the auditorium.

A lady goes up to the mic. "I agree with him. Where is the respect?" She sits down.

Nobody moves for a few seconds. I don't want this woman's words to be the last thing the board hears. I lean down to gather my note cards to see if there's something else I can add, but out of the corner of my eye, I see Olivia get up. She stands in front of Pearl, who reaches out and grabs her hand.

"Hi," Olivia says softly. "I'm Olivia. Some people call me 'Tampon Fail.' It's okay. I'm used to it. So I went shopping over spring break with my aunt and bought these white pants I couldn't wait to wear. I put them on and felt so confident walking into school with my new pants and my UCLA sweatshirt."

"Yeah, UCLA," Jasmine yells out.

Olivia smiles. "I got up after math class, and my friend Pearl over here did what friends should always do. She told me I had my period, and it was on the back of my pants. I panicked and tied my sweatshirt around my waist and went to call my sister. But Dr. Couchman stopped me for wearing a tank top. He made me go out to the garden and told me I had ruined the class trip for the entire eighth grade. The rest is history. I just want to thank Molly Frost and all the people who stood up for me. This could have been the worst month of my life. But instead, it was the best."

Enough is enough.

THE THING ABOUT SOULS

Remember those tiny pieces, the bits that break off and burn off and fly away?

I have good news. They can come back.

YEARBOOK DAY

Will and I are in the tree house. It seems empty without our signs, which are sitting in a pile in the back of our mini-van waiting to be paraded through the streets if we hear bad news from the board of education. We flip through our yearbooks, laughing at how young we looked at the beginning of the year.

"What would you write next to your picture now?" Will asks.

"You mean instead of 'lacrosse, clarinet, and all kinds of music'? That's not interesting enough for you?" I dig around my backpack for a good yearbook-signing pen. "I think I would write 'Enough is enough' and have my grandchildren try to figure out what that means fifty years from now."

"I'd write 'Pearl is not your grandma.'"

"Good one."

The last day of school was bizarre. Dr. Couchman and Fingertip were both out "sick." Mrs. Peabody told everyone they had hand, foot, and mouth disease and that it's very contagious, so everyone should wash their hands.

"I think it's a bad case of hand-foot-*in*-mouth disease," Will says, scrolling through my phone, reading the many plays on words happening in our group text.

LETTER LETTER LETTER LETTER, Liza texts.
She posts it on @DressCodedAPodcast.

Dear Parents,

The board of education has reviewed the comments and letters we've received both from last night's emergency meeting and via email. We appreciate the input and the community attention to this matter.

While all the comments were compelling, a couple of things stood out. First, the high school has never enforced its dress code, and apart from the very rare hate-speech incidents that require immediate action, students and faculty have been content ignoring the dress code. Next, we were especially concerned that a number of people shared stories and photographs of two or more students wearing the exact same outfit with very different outcomes. Enforcement of the dress code at Fisher Middle School was not, in fact, consistent.

And finally, our district will not tolerate discrimination in any form. The fact that a young woman was punished after a young man touched her hair is both disturbing and unacceptable. We will be implementing some programming and personnel changes, effective immediately.

I can assure you we take this matter very seriously. We apologize for letting this escape our attention in the past and for the interim super-

intendent's lack of attention to the student petition. After much deliberation, we have decided
with a vote of 5–2 to remove the school dress code
from the FMS and FHS student handbooks. We
will rewrite the dress code over the summer with
input from the young women who spearheaded this
effort. Special thanks to those young women, to
all of you for making your voices heard, and to Ms.
Susanna Milholland for her wisdom and guidance.

Have a safe and joyful summer.

Mae Dunn, MPH, MD
Chair, Board of Education

PRINCESS MOLLIFLOWER AND PRINCE WILLISTER HAVE MUCH TO CELEBRATE

Will jumps up and down. He bangs his head on the tree-house ceiling, and I text Mom to bring us an ice pack. **But check your email first.**

She runs out, forgets the ice pack, runs back in, and then looks really awkward trying to get into the tree house.

"You did it, Molly," she says with tears in her eyes. "I'm really proud of you."

"Me too," Will says.

"I'm proud of us," I say. I reread the letter aloud. "I hope the 'programming and personnel changes' involve reprogramming some personalities."

Mom goes inside to call everyone she knows to tell them about me and my mission accomplished. It must feel good to brag about a kid, after so much time spent crying and complaining about Danny.

Will holds the ice pack on his head, and we wait for everyone to get here so we can celebrate.

"You never did a podcast," I say.

"I'll do one if I ever get dress coded."

"Okay. It's a deal."

MIDDLE SCHOOL IS NOT *THAT* BAD

- Getting an A on a test you thought you failed
- Trick-or-treating with oversize pillowcases
- Sledding on snow days
- Field trips and jamborees
- Learning something you'll actually use someday
- Pizza Fridays
- Staying up past midnight on your birthday to see all your friends' birthday wishes on Snapchat
- Wearing your favorite outfit
- Scoring a goal
- Having a week, a day, a moment with your mom or dad that feels like old times
- Playing board games with your brother
- Making new best friends
- Reconnecting with old best friends
- Getting candy from the kid next to you in class when you're really, really hungry
- Hearing a teacher say, "Wow. That was awesome."
- Hearing a parent say, "Wow. That was awesome."
- Saying to yourself, "Wow. That was awesome."
- Walks to get ice cream

- A smile from a high school kid on the bus
- Long Saturday sleeps
- Half days
- Movies in class
- Squeezing too many adult-size bodies into a child-size tree house for giant quantities of junk food and a lot of hugging and singing
- Knowing that the best times are still to come
- Making your voice heard
- Knowing that voice is yours forever

DANNY'S LETTER

Dear Molly,

I got your letter. You're a better writer than me. I know I've been a bad brother. I'm sorry. (Not even kidding—I'm really sorry.) You're a solid kid. Stay that way. I'm going to go to Granny's because she'll get me in shape. That's because she's not afraid to grab my ear and twist it. (Not a joke.) I'll see you soon. If you need me to come back and kick some boy's butt for you, I will. But I'm pretty sure you are capable of kicking butt.

Love,
Dan

Mom and Dad line us all up for photos in front of the rosebushes in Violeta's garden.

We smile and pose and make faces, and more families show up to make sure we get photographic evidence that we all survived middle school.

"Just you and Will," Will's mom says.

"Hurry up, Mom. This is embarrassing." Will fake-smiles in his khakis and button-down shirt with a tie.

"That's a gorgeous dress, Molly," Will's mom says.

It should be, for the original price of $425.

I work up a sweat trying to corral my friends for a picture. A month ago, it would have been easy: just Navya, Ashley, Bea, and me. But now, after everything, I need them all here in the garden. We need a picture together in our white dresses.

Navya, Bea, and me. Megan Birch. Liza, Pearl, and Olivia. Mary Kate and Lucy, who are on the Moving Up Day committee, and Talia, who is getting ready to sing a solo.

"Ready?" I ask Bea and Navya.

"Yep," Navya says, walking toward the side doors.

"Hold on a second," Pearl says. She walks up behind Will and taps him on the shoulder. He turns around and looks a little startled. She whispers something in his ear and lifts her hand up for a high five. He smiles and rushes to catch up with Chen.

Bea and Pearl talked before the emergency meeting. After two minutes of awkward, they spent twenty minutes talking about K-pop. This is all good, because we're planning a campout (as opposed to a camp-in), and it won't be fun if everyone is avoiding each other.

"Where's Dan?" Liza asks.

"Home."

"Sorry."

"No, it's okay. I asked him to stay home. I really didn't want him sitting there with all the eighth graders who learned to vape because of him."

"True."

We file into the cafeteria, and sour-faced Dr. Couchman greets each of us with a handshake. He's as bad as Ashley's mom at hiding his hatred for kids.

Nick huddles with his minions. I wonder if he'll grow up a little over the summer or if he'll continue trying to assign nicknames to people who will be too busy to care about his nonsense.

We stand in groups, waiting to go to the gym. The seventh-grade choir is singing, and I'm cheering on Talia, who says she's never nervous onstage.

"Please line up," Dr. Couchman says with his teeth clenched. "Mrs. Aeyler will be handing out programs."

"Who is Mrs. Aeyler?" Bea asks.

"Fingertip," I say, nodding toward the dean of nobody-knows-what-now-because-she-won't-be-allowed-to-torment-girls-next-year.

"Wow, their hand, foot, and mouth disease has magically disappeared," Megan says.

I run over to Ashley and tap her on the shoulder. "Hey, Ash. You look so pretty."

"So do you, Moll."

It feels weird, and I wonder if this is the way it will always be. Who knows what high school will bring?

We file into the gym and sit in rows in the middle, surrounded by our parents, who are all waving programs in front of their faces because it's brutally hot.

If we didn't know who Mae Dunn was a week ago, we do now. The interim superintendent, who *still* hasn't addressed our petition, asks the board of education to stand. We rise to our feet and cheer.

Thank you, I mouth to Ms. Lane, who is sitting on the bleachers nearby.

We sit and focus our eyes on the teachers giving sports awards (*Go, Navya! Trophy queen!*), academic awards (*Go, Olivia! Science queen!*), service awards (*Go, community service club!*), art awards (*Go, Bea!*), writing awards (*Liza and Pearl, obviously*), and music awards (*Well done, Tom!*), and we pretend sweat isn't drenching every inch of our bodies. We cheer for our friends and our classmates, and think about ice-cold showers.

I tap Megan on the shoulder. "You get the Molly-Passed-Science-Because-of-Me Award," I whisper. She nods enthusiastically.

"Before we close," Ms. Santos-Skinner says, "I've invited Pearl Park to read one of her poems. She happened to choose my favorite."

Pearl's hands tremble as she stands. She steps up to the podium, leans over the microphone, and in her soft, beautiful Pearl voice, she reads.

Olivia's Tears

When Olivia's tears fell to the ground
The skies darkened
The birds went silent
The bugs felt pain
As they often do

And then in defiance
A single tear grew
Molecule by molecule

Until it was bigger than me
Until it was bigger than you

It cleansed the silk of the moth's cocoon
It softened the thorns of the tea-rose bush
And the bumblebee sipped to feed her young
And the chickadee stretched her glistening wings
And the spider washed her cluttered web
And the chipmunk bathed her weary feet

Look what one tear has done
Look what one tear can do

ALL'S WELL IN BEARVILLE: A PODCAST

MARY KATE: Hello, Fisher Middle School and beyond. This is Mary Kate Murphy, and I'm taking over Molly Frost's podcast, formerly known as *Dress Coded*, because Molly is going to high school and we both agree Fisher could still use a podcast. I'm calling the new podcast *All's Well in Bearville*, and I'm going to interview anyone who wants to talk about issues important to them. I will definitely be talking about endangered species a lot, because that's my issue, but first I'm going to focus on doing whatever it takes to stop bear hunting in our state. There are plenty of ways to control the bear population without murdering them. That I know for sure.

Today we're doing a follow-up on everything that happened to successfully replace the Fisher Middle School dress code in the student handbook. I was on the committee to rewrite the dress code for the upcoming school year. Here with me now is fellow committee member Molly Frost. Congratulations, Molly. How do you feel?

MOLLY: I'm really happy we made it happen before we went to high school so you and your friends and the incoming seventh graders can start school without worrying about the dress code.

MARY KATE: I agree. Thank you for everything, Molly.

MOLLY: Thank *you*. You were brave joining us, knowing you were going to have to go to that school for another year.

MARY KATE: Now that you pretty much know how to change something you view as unfair, do you think you'll be changing stuff at the high school?

MOLLY: Hmm. Great question. *[Pauses.]* I have a feeling there will be things, bigger things beyond high school, but I think we'll probably start by helping people from other districts fight their unfair dress codes.

MARY KATE: That's a good idea. Do you have any advice for the incoming seventh graders entering FMS?

MOLLY: I would say that middle school isn't always easy. Friendships are different every week, and that's okay. The work can be stressful, but you'll get used to it. And sometimes you might wake up in the middle of the night and feel horrible about yourself because you don't like the shape of your body or the constellation of pimples on your face that appeared out of nowhere. Those feelings will come and go. But now, at least you can wear something comfortable and not worry about people criticizing you and making you feel even more self-conscious.

MARY KATE: Exactly.

MOLLY: I'd also say that the boys get a bad rap. We know you are just as self-conscious as we are, and now you can go to school and sit in class without somebody accusing you of being distracted by a shoulder or a collarbone or a leg.

MARY KATE: That's a good point. Anything else?

MOLLY: Just remember, you have Ms. Lane and Mr. Beam

and Ms. Santos-Skinner and Mrs. Tucker and Mr. Lu. When you're struggling, look to the light. They're the light. Oh, and don't vape.

MARY KATE: Yeah, incoming seventh graders, vaping is disgusting.

MOLLY: We're here if you need us, FMS. High school kids aren't as scary as they look. I promise.

MARY KATE: Thank you, Molly. We love you.

MOLLY: I love you too, Fisher Middle School.

THE AMENDED FISHER MIDDLE SCHOOL DRESS CODE

<u>Students must wear:</u>

— Top (shirt, sweater, or dress);

— Bottom (pants, sweatpants, shorts, skirt, dress, or leggings); and

— Shoes (including proper footwear for science lab and gym class).

<u>Students may not wear:</u>

— Clothing that depicts hate speech, profanity, or illegal, lewd, or violent activity.

Other than that, you be you.

ACKNOWLEDGMENTS

I am grateful to the women and girls who inspired, informed, and believed in this book. You are the fireflies who lit the story's path:

Emily Firestone
Lauren Firestone
Lindsay Snyder
Juli Berrio
Marissa Blaha
Jordan DuBois
Ella Young
Dana Barcellos-Allen
Alissa Mills
Lashantee Crawley
Tanya Contois
Callista DeGraw
Sabrina DeGraw
Madison Edwards
Lisa Levinger
Gabi Levinger-Louie
Margaux Levinger-Louie
Vicki Judd
Taylor Armstrong

Anna Szekeres
Mary Wirpel
Jestina Gilbert
Amanda Finman

Thanks to our school district in Avon, Connecticut—
Dr. Bridget Carnemolla, Laura Young, Jackie Blea, and
Debi Chute—for showing us what a dress code *should*
look like.

Thank you to #TeamEleni, ForwardCT, and our fear-
less leader, Eleni Kavros DeGraw, for showing us what the
best of community *can* look like.

Thanks to Leora Tanenbaum for @BeingDressCoded
and Laura Orsi and Clara Mitchell for starting the powerful
#PassTheSkirt movement.

Thank you, Denise Alfeld, the Pandas, and all my writer
friends.

Thank you to my family and BFFs for your unwavering
love and encouragement all these years.

Thank you to Sara Crowe, queen of the fireflies, and the
amazing Pippin team for always having my back. Thank
you to Stephanie Pitts for your insight, brilliance, and hard
work, Jen Klonsky and the Putnam team for your support and enthusiasm, Tyler Feder for your beautiful art,
Maggie Edkins for the cover design, and Suki Boynton for
the interior design.

And thank you, Michael Firestone, for living with three
strong women (four, if you count Roxie) and always being
on our side.

In the 1850s, a small group of reformers began to argue

against the restrictive clothing women of that era were forced to wear. As a result, they were taunted, judged, and condemned. But they persisted. They set the stage for decades of dress reform movements to come. They showed us that it is unjust to control, intimidate, humiliate, and silence women simply for wearing what feels comfortable. To the brave voices that galvanized future generations to fight for justice for ALL women—this book is for you.

**READ ON FOR MORE FROM
CARRIE FIRESTONE**

THE LETTER THAT STARTS IT ALL

Dear Parent or Guardian,

I am pleased to announce that Fisher Middle School has received a generous grant to fund a climate science pilot program this year. The class will explore how and why climate change is happening and how we can use community-based projects to take action.

Out of over a hundred application essays students submitted in March, the following rising eighth graders have been selected to participate:

Elijah Campbell
Shawn Hill
Benjamin Lettle
Andrew Limski
Jay Mendes
Rabia Mohammed
Mary Kate Murphy
Lucy Perlman
Rebecca Phelps
Hannah Small

Warning! This class will be a lot of work. Please talk to your child and make sure they're ready to commit. We

will still cover standard eighth-grade science concepts,
but this class is not going to be "traditional." If you
and your child are on board, please sign and return the
attached form. Congratulations to all the students!
   I can't wait to get started.

                                    Scientifically yours,
                                    Ed Lu

My climate-class acceptance letter is stuck to the refrigerator door with an E magnet, next to a picture of my new baby niece, Penelope, and a Post-it reminding Dad to buy more back-pain cream.

All the inspirational E magnet words aren't working for me right now, because I'm not *eager* or *enthusiastic* or *excited* about school starting tomorrow. My best friend, Lucy, has been sick the whole summer, and nobody knows what's wrong with her. I would have been eager, enthusiastic, and excited to be in the climate class with Lucy. Instead, I'm going to be sitting with a group of kids I barely know.

I text Lucy: **Fairy village?** But she doesn't text back, which means she's sleeping, having a really sick day, or mad at me for even asking.

I'm almost thirteen years old, and I'm going to build a fairy house by myself. But Lucy and I promised each other we would do it every year the day before school starts, for good luck, and we really need the good luck right now. So I put on my shoes, call my dogs, Murphy and Claudia, to come with me, grab my backpack, and walk out the back door.

My backyard and Lucy's backyard are separated by a huge nature preserve, which was donated to our town by a family who must have had a crystal ball and seen that if you don't specifically say *This piece of land can never be used for anything but enjoying nature*, it will eventually turn into a Dunkin' Donuts, a car dealership, or a nail salon.

Not many people visit the preserve, probably because there aren't really trails. It's one huge chunk of beautiful land, with a sledding hill, and a meadow, and a pond, and a vernal pool in spring, and crumbling old stone walls, and woods surrounding it all.

I walk around our barn, which is now a big garage with an upstairs room, follow the path through the woods to the top of the sledding hill, and cut through the sunflowers at the edge of the meadow.

Most people wouldn't notice the fairy village if they made their way into the woods. It looks like some creature randomly dropped piles of bark and twigs. But we know. Lucy and I and the fairies have a lot of secrets hidden here.

When we were younger, we spent entire days collecting pine cones, and lost feathers, and interesting stones, and acorns, and fallen flower petals. We built fancy fairy houses and did all kinds of fairy-summoning rituals I can't remember anymore. But I don't feel like doing any of that. Right now, I want to build a house, get the good luck, and go home.

I pick up a few sturdy sticks and lean them against a fallen trunk that's covered in moss. I leave a space for the fairies to come and go, and cover the little lean-to with soft pine needles. I drop stones around the house and scatter handfuls of leaves on the roof.

It's not our best house, but it's good enough.

Sleep well, fairies, I wish. *And please bring us luck.*

ON THE BUS

My neighbor Molly and I have been sitting together on the bus since I was in kindergarten and she was in first grade. We used to get harassed by Molly's older brother, Danny, who calls us Frog and Toad for some reason, but Danny is living with his grandma in New York, so Frog and Toad have a break this year.

"Do you like my tank top?" I ask, sliding into the seat across from my other neighbor, Will.

"I *love* your tank top," Molly says. "It really emphasizes those shoulders."

"Thank you, my queen," I say, because I'm very grateful that Molly and her friends started a protest against our school's dress code this past June, which ended with the school district letting us wear pretty much whatever we want.

"Remember how scared you were when school started last year?" Molly says, eating a granola bar. "I thought you were going to throw up."

"I wasn't looking forward to seventh grade."

What Molly doesn't know is that I wasn't scared. I was annoyed. I didn't know how I was going to go from an entire summer of frogging and tree climbing to being pushed down a crowded hallway eight times a day.

"I'm going to miss seeing you," Molly says. "Now I'm the one about to throw up. The high school has way too many people I don't know. Say something to distract me."

"Like what?"

"I don't know. Tell me about the podcast. Are you still going to do it?"

"I doubt it."

"Why not? It was really good."

I don't feel like talking about *Bearsville* with Molly. It's embarrassing.

Will shoves his phone in our faces to show us his summer-camp girlfriend, and Molly spends the rest of the bus ride asking him questions he doesn't know the answers to.

"Do you think you'll see her before next summer?"

"I don't know."

"Is she going to camp next summer?"

"I don't know."

The bus stops in front of the high school, and Molly makes an *ughhh* sound.

"You've got this, Molls," I say. "You're a queen, remember?"

Will and Molly jump off the bus, and Molly runs over to her friends Navya and Bea. I watch them go into the high school as the bus rolls out of the circle toward Fisher Middle School.

FAILURE TO LAUNCH

I tried to start a podcast this summer. It was called *All's Well in Bearville*, but I changed it to *All's Well in Bearsville* after the first episode because there's a lot more than one bear in this town. It was supposed to be about why bear hunting in our state is inhumane, and how to deal with climate change, and interesting nature stories.

The *Bearsville* idea came from Molly, who used a podcast to start the dress-code protest, and then *Dress Coded: A Podcast* ended up inspiring people all over the country to fight their school dress codes.

Bearsville, on the other hand, never really went anywhere.

Maybe it was because the state had already passed a law banning bear hunting, or because the people I interviewed used a lot of science words. My cousin in Florida said the interview with the professor about climate change and frogs was "kind of boring." My other cousin said the questions I asked the tree expert were "too smart." Molly said, "It's really well done, Mary Kate, but people have a lot going on in the summer."

One of my mom's regular customers at the bookstore looked at the *Bearsville* flyer on the bulletin board and said, "I'm more of a book person than a podcast person."

The only people who actually listened to all three episodes were my ninety-one-year-old grandmother and her roommate, Linda, in Florida, and Lucy, who gave me a lot of content ideas.

Then Lucy got sick, I got distracted, and it was easy to let go of something that had only three listeners. It might have been different if I could have actually interviewed the bears, the frogs, and the trees.

Lucy texts right as the bus is turning down the long Fisher Middle School driveway: **On the way to another 'ologist. Come over after school. Good luck.**

Lucy started acting strange at the end of school last year.

At first, I thought she was mad at me. Every time I asked her to meet at the pond, she said she didn't feel good and needed to take a nap. Then I was afraid she was getting sick of me, or that she maybe wanted to go hang out with her basketball friends. But then I heard my mom on the phone with her mom.

"Have you tested her for anemia?"

"What about blood sugar issues?"

"I mean, narcolepsy, but the symptoms don't add up."

"Why would she think her food was contaminated? That's so odd. You're right. It does sound like anxiety."

It got worse. Every time I went to her house, all she wanted to do was sleep. Then she felt better for a while, at least good enough to go down to the pond one afternoon and wait for the bats to come out. Lucy is obsessed with bats. But even then, her legs hurt, and she had shooting pains in random places and squishy sounds in her ears and blurry vision and a burning tongue. And she was constantly worried about bugs getting in her mouth, so she didn't want to talk.

"I'm going home to sleep a little," she said. "I'll be back for the bats."

She was never back for the bats.

Lucy went to a psychiatrist (a mental health doctor) because she doesn't want to do anything or talk to anyone, and she's not herself *at all*. They gave her anxiety medicine that hasn't helped.

She went to a neurologist (a brain doctor) because she's forgetting words and now she has a thing where she jerks her arms and blinks her eyes over and over again.

Then a gastroenterologist (a stomach doctor) because onions and milk and a lot of other foods make her nauseated.

And a rheumatologist (a joint doctor) because her whole body hurts.

Nobody knows what's wrong with Lucy.

Today she's going to a urologist. She doesn't know that I know, but I overheard my mom talking to her mom again. It's scary and embarrassing, and I'll never tell anyone, but Lucy has been wetting the bed.

Before the last 'ologist appointment, Lucy said, "No matter what, Mare, I'm going to school. I'm not making you walk into that place alone."

That was a week ago. "No matter what" has come and gone.

THAT PLACE

"That place" is Fisher Middle School, which seems smaller today, for some reason.

The bus stops in front of the school, and I catch up with Talia, who is sitting a couple rows in front of me, before getting off. Then we follow everyone to the Kindness Garden, where Fisher students drop rocks with inspiring words painted on them before they start seventh grade. My word was so boring, I don't even remember it.

The new superintendent, Dr. Eastman, bursts out of the office wearing a black jumpsuit and yellow high heels and carrying a LET'S MAKE MAGIC THIS YEAR sign. She has strong witch vibes, and I like it.

She introduces our new principal, Ms. Singh, who has smiled more in the past three minutes than our old principal did in a year.

"Dr. Eastman seems so nice," Talia says. "I like her Southern accent."

Talia was part of the dress-code protest last year, which a lot of people think was the thing that drove out the old principal and his sidekick, a woman we called Fingertip. I'm pretty sure they're right.

"And this, friends, is Mr. Joe, our new dean of students," the superintendent says, putting her hand on Mr.

Joe's shoulder. "Is somebody giving you a hard time? Are you having a tough interpersonal issue? If so, go to Joe."

I give Talia a good-luck hug, find my locker, then walk to gym, where we introduce ourselves and say one thing we did over the summer: "I'm Mary Kate Murphy, and I visited my sister, Sarah, in Boston and met my new baby niece, Penelope." In math, we throw a ball of yarn around the class and have to say a fun fact about ourselves when we catch it. Wow. Now I know Ben Lettle's favorite color is brown.

I'm on my way to English when I run into big block letters that say CONGRATULATIONS TO OUR CLIMATE CLASS FOR THESE WINNING ESSAYS. Somebody thought it would be a good idea to hang our climate-class application essays on a bulletin board. Now the whole school can read about my weirdness whenever they walk by.

CLIMATE CLASS APPLICATION ESSAY

MARY KATE MURPHY

We always hear about climate change and polar bears, and that's very upsetting and devastating, because polar bears are starving to death and turning to cannibalism. But I want to talk about the bears that live in my backyard.

Most people don't realize how many bears live in the middle of Connecticut. Our town has more bears than nearly any other town. I observe them all the time, especially a few different families that have been coming around for a while.

When I was little, the bears would always feed in this area of the Honey Hill Preserve that had a lot of wild blackberry bushes. I'm only twelve, but just in my lifetime I've seen the bushes ripening earlier and earlier with fewer and fewer berries. The bears have to look for other sources of food, and that means they are going to garbage cans and ending up on Facebook posts with people complaining about how annoying the bears are, which makes people want to start shooting them.

If you do an online search of nearly any plant or animal on Earth and then "climate change impact," you'll see ways entire ecosystems are being disrupted by climate change. But I don't need to look it up because I see it with my own eyes, with blackberries, bears, salamanders and frogs, plants and bees and butterflies. I'm not exaggerating. It's all changing every year.

If you accept me into the climate class, I would like to learn more about the changes I'm seeing in my backyard and how to stop them before all the creatures I actually care about are gone, because I consider these creatures my friends.

I'm still trying to get used to having only eight students in English class. There was a problem with the schedule, and now the people in my English class third period are the same people in my climate class eighth period. There's supposed to be ten of us, but Lucy is sick and Andrew Limski was forced to drop out of the pilot program because, according to Jay, his parents didn't think the climate class sounded challenging enough.

I watch everyone come in and sit in the circle of desks.

Ben Lettle grew a half mustache over the summer. Maybe his parents don't think he's ready to handle a razor. I get it. The bathtub scene whenever I try to shave my legs looks like the time Dad tried to blend tomatoes and forgot to put the top on the blender.

Elijah Campbell is wearing a bumblebee bow tie.

Shawn Hill grew, like, a foot since seventh grade and got glasses.

Rabia Mohammed's wearing the shoes I wanted, but Dad said what he always says: "That's too steep for our budget."

Jay Mendes has a green bruise on his forehead from playing soccer. (That was his fun fact in math.)

Hannah Small and Rebecca Phelps are whispering. This is eighth-grade code for *We hung out together at the pool club over the summer, and now we have secrets.*

Our English teacher, Ms. Lane, takes attendance. Ms. Lane has always been just Charlotte to me. She was one of the first people on earth I ever met. She and my sister, Sarah, who happens to be eighteen years older than me, have been best friends most of their lives, and Sarah brought Charlotte to the hospital after I was born to meet me.

"Today we begin our letter-writing project," Ms. Lane says.

"Seriously? Pen pals again?" Elijah says. "They literally never write back."

"No, not pen pals, Elijah." She goes to her desk, pulls a folded piece of yellow lined paper from her bag, and starts to read:

Dear Charlotte,

I really miss summer vacation. Ms. Milholland is making us write letters to ourselves, which seems weird, but whatever. She says she's not going to read the letters and they're for us to keep and read when we grow up. I trust her. She's pretty cool. I'm making an announcement that I haven't even told Sarah. I think I'm in love with Greg Johnson. Like, he's as perfect as a boy can be. He's got dimples, and he's taller than me. He's kind of like Leonardo DiCaprio from Titanic, *but hotter. Why does he have to be sixteen? Why is life so unfair? Bell ringing.*

Love
Me

We stare at her.

"That, my friends, was classic Ms. Lane in eighth grade. And I'm sharing it with you because, as embarrassing as it is, I adore these letters. I should also point out there's no comma between 'Love' and 'Me,' which is a good example of how a comma changes everything."

"Oh, I get it," Rebecca says, laughing.

"Ms. Milholland made us write a letter to ourselves every month the entire year, and, whoa—the drama, the failed romance, the puberty complaints. It was nice to get it all down on paper and let it go," Ms. Lane says. "You're next. You're going to write a letter to yourselves at the beginning of every month for the whole school year. I'll collect the letters, but I won't read them. You have my word. I have enough drama in my life."

Hannah raises her hand. "Where's Greg Johnson now?"

Ms. Lane smiles. "I have no idea. I think that crush only lasted until the next letter. So, you have your homework assignment. Let's move on to poetry. My favorite."

"Ms. Lane, who are they going to get to replace you if you win the election?" Elijah asks. "It's in November, right?"

Ms. Lane is also running for mayor of our town, against a guy named Brent Grimley, who has been the mayor my entire life—and, according to my parents, has accomplished absolutely nothing.

Ms. Lane laughs. "Yes, Election Day is always the first Tuesday in November. I appreciate all the interest around my campaign, including the suggestion from another class that we turn my classroom into my campaign headquarters, but I'm making a firm rule: no discussing the campaign in school. I don't think it's appropriate."

She writes *No Election Talk!* in cursive on a giant hot-pink Post-it and sticks it to the board.

"They're going to get Mr. Linkler, the sub, aren't they?" Elijah says.

"Okay, last thing I'll say is that *if* I were to win, it's a part-time job. So I'll still be your devoted teacher."

"Oh, wow. Mayor is definitely not part-time in Hartford," Shawn says.

"That's because they have a lot of crime in Hartford," Ben says.

"Okay, Ben," Shawn says. "That's why."

"Well, isn't that why the Hartford kids want to go to school here?" Ben asks.

Shawn is one of the Hartford kids.

"You know better than to say something like that, Ben," Ms. Lane says.

"Like what?" Ben says.

"Let's move on," Ms. Lane says, shaking her head.